JAMAICA
MISTAICA

A JAKE SULLIVAN NOVEL

THE JAKE SULLIVAN SERIES

Come Monday

Trying to Reason with Hurricane Season

Havana Daydreamin'

A Pirate Looks at Forty

One Particular Harbour

Son of a Son of a Sailor

Jamaica Mistaica

ALSO AVAILABLE:

Trilogy

COMING SPRING 2016:

Changes in Latitudes, Changes in Attitudes

JAMAICA MISTAICA

A JAKE SULLIVAN NOVEL

CHIP BELL

WORD ASSOCIATION PUBLISHERS
www.wordassociation.com
1.800.827.7903

Printed in the United States of America.

ISBN: 978-1-63385-065-1

Library of Congress Control Number: 2015915446

Designed and published by

Word Association Publishers
205 Fifth Avenue
Tarentum, Pennsylvania 15084

www.wordassociation.com
1.800.827.7903

"Come back, come back

Back to Jamaica

Don't you know we made a big Mistaica

We'd be so sad if you told us goodbye

And we promise not to shoot you out of the sky."

- "Jamaica Mistaica"
by Jimmy Buffett

To SSG Mack Owens, United States Army, Retired . . . "The Boss".
One of the best men I have ever known. He made me a better man
than I otherwise would have been.

ACKNOWLEDGEMENT

To all the wonderful folks out there who have been so kind to read my books. I hope you enjoy this one and all that follow.

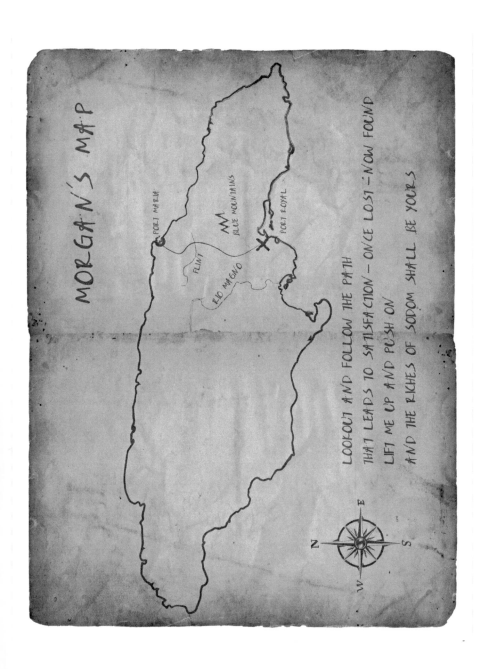

MORGAN'S MAP

PORT MARIA

FLINT

RIO MAGNO

BLUE MOUNTAINS

PORT ROYAL

LOOKOUT AND FOLLOW THE PATH
THAT LEADS TO SATISFACTION — ONCE LOST — NOW FOUND
LIFT ME UP AND PUSH ON
AND THE RICHES OF SODOM SHALL BE YOURS

PROLOGUE

THE PIRATE

CHAPTER 1

May 1688

The flint-eyed individual worked tirelessly over the pieces of parchment on the desk before him in the stone observation point. Finally, he set down his quill pen and noticed the flicker of the candle flame that provided light for his endeavors. It jumped and danced like one of the girls he had romanced as a younger man, in Cartagena. He smiled to himself, thinking of all that he had been through, and how, now, finally, he was ready to reap the rewards of his efforts.

Just then, the pain struck, stabbing like a knife at his midsection, like it always did, causing him to double over and grimace as he rose and walked outside to stand on the bluff, looking out over the Windward Passage and the lights of Port Maria below.

The cool night air always seemed to lessen the pain, and even though he had his vast estates in Lawrencefield and elsewhere on the island, he came here more and more often, as the pain had increased over the last few months.

He eased himself onto a bench and looked into the night, knowing that to the east the Passage continued between Cuba and

Hispaniola, providing the gateway to both the New and the Old Worlds for all the wealth that flowed from the lands and islands of the Caribbean Sea.

He remembered how he had fought long and hard to make his superiors understand the strategic significance of this island, Jamaica, and he had been with the force that had invaded and taken it from Spain.

He chuckled to himself, "Ah, yes. Spain." How they hated him there. He took pride in that hate and knew that it was no boast to claim he was the most famous, or some would say infamous, privateer of his day, wreaking havoc on the Spanish along the Spanish Main, the whole way to Panama, and through all the islands of the Caribbean.

They had come to realize it was better to have him as a friend than as an enemy, so long as he was willing to pay the price of that friendship. He had known long ago that it would come to this, and that's why he had planned and worked for years to bring about this moment.

The pain was almost gone and he got up and walked, still unsteady on his feet, to the hole in the ground that was the beginning of a passage that led down to the beach at Port Maria. He had told his men it was an escape route, but it was much more than that.

He had started in May of 1670, bringing in crews and sending them with the guides he had hired into the caves that ran underneath all of Jamaica. He had learned as a young man about the cave system that lay at the foot of the Blue Mountains with its tall chambers and many passages, and he had his men create a secret entrance into the system and connect those passages to create a route from Port Maria the whole way to Port Royal.

It was only when the job was completed at the end of 1670 that he set sail for the City of Panama, marching through the jungle and attacking it from the rear in January of 1671, burning it to the ground. The rumors he, himself, had started, that most of the silver, jewels, and gold for which Panama was famous, had been taken to sea by its inhabitants when they had learned that he was coming, were false. The truth was that he had separate crews on separate ships the whole time, and those crews marched the majority of the wealth of Panama back by a different route to those ships. He had run his flagship, the Satisfaction, and four other ships aground on the reefs to the entrance of the Chagres River after he had destroyed the fortress of San Lorenzo to create the belief that he had no way to bring a sizable fortune back to Jamaica.

After Panama City had been destroyed, he brought his crew back to the mouth of the river and had them occupy San Lorenzo, and while they did so, he sailed away into the night, knowing full well they would be slaughtered by the Spanish reinforcements that were coming to Panama.

The two ships full of plunder sailed into Port Maria late at night, and their crew used the darkness to unload the vast riches of Panama and loaded them into the secret system of tunnels that he had created.

For days thereafter, his men moved the treasure through the tunnel system to the warehouse he had constructed, under a different name, in Port Royal.

It was only then that he sailed into Port Royal with a small portion of the plunder to the acclaim of all.

For a moment he again gazed at the leaping flame of the candle and closed his eyes.

"No," he thought to himself, "I will not do it. I will not feel guilt. I will not feel remorse." The men at San Lorenzo had to die, just as the entire crews that created the passages and moved the treasure to the warehouse had to die, buried alive in one of the caves, just as his faithful first mate, Bartholomew, had to die at the very end, so no one, no one but he, would know the secret of the treasure from Panama.

He had bided his time, consolidating his power, establishing himself in Jamaican society, and cultivating his wealthy landowner persona for over fifteen years. Now he was ready to act.

And now, that treasure would pay the Spanish price and secure his goal. Soon the documents would be completed and he would be Governor General of the Caribbean, completely in charge of the islands of Cuba and Hispaniola and Jamaica, which he would take by armed force, if necessary, along with the lands of the Spanish Main. He had convinced the Spanish that their possessions in the New World would be much more profitable with him overseeing the safety of their shipments, rather than attacking them.

He was sure he could convince London to follow suit, to give him the same title and control of their possessions and trade routes, ending years of conflict and giving everyone the prosperity of peace.

Some would call him a traitor, but he scoffed at the idea. They had sent him to London in irons after the raid on Panama, and he returned as Acting Governor. Those who sat far away and attempted to rule were fools. He, and he alone, knew what must be done in the Caribbean, and soon the power would be his.

He rubbed his eyes. He was getting tired. His carriage had arrived, and he knew it was near midnight . . . time for him to return to Lawrencefield. He finished the last pages he was working on, picked up the leather case that contained all the documents and agreements of his plan, and stood, ready to conceal them in their hiding place, but before he did, he took out a piece of folded leather and opened it and looked at it by the light of the candle and smiled.

"Poor Bartholomew," he thought. "The man made masterful charts, but this, his last creation, was a study in simplicity."

"'Morgan's Map,' the key to it all," he thought. It would take a quick mind to figure it out, but only a quick mind warranted the wealth and power it bestowed.

He hid the leather case with the folded piece of leather and the documents where he always did, blew out the candle, and went out to his carriage.

"Time to go home, Jonathan," he said to the driver. As he stepped up into the carriage, the pain came again, this time worse than before. The pain would continue and increase over the next three months and by August 1688, the great Henry Morgan would be dead, and his plans for the Caribbean would die with him.

CHAPTER 2

June 1692

Isaac, a boy of thirteen, had been sent by his master to Port Royal to pick up new harnesses he had ordered at the blacksmith shop for his team of plow horses.

As he always did, Isaac took a long route to the blacksmith's and back to his master's estate. He loved to walk down on the wharf to see the ships sailing in and out of the harbor and to see the pirates, famous and not, who strolled along the streets. For the past thirty years, Port Royal had become a pirate utopia and was known as the "Sodom of the New World". Most of its residents were pirates or prostitutes or tavern owners, with a ratio of one drinking house for every ten residents. In 1692, there were almost 6,500 people living in the city, making it second only to Boston as the largest city in the New World. There were over 2,000 buildings crammed into 51 acres of real estate and over 200 ships visited the port each year. The wealth of Port Royal was signified by the fact that coins were required for services and barter did not exist.

But piracy was on the wane. After the appointment of Henry Morgan as Lieutenant Governor, anti-piracy laws were passed in

1687 and notables, such as Charles Vane and Calico Jack Rackham would be hanged in gibbets on Gallows Point in the years to come.

Isaac sighed to himself, as he knew it was time to go fetch the harnesses and go home. He took a shortcut through one of the alleys and found himself at the water's edge, beside a flat, one-story square structure that he had noticed before. He walked around it several times, still trying to understand why it had no doors nor windows, and why there were never any signs of movement around it. Finally, he shook his head, unable to understand, and headed to the blacksmith shop to complete his chore.

The blacksmith was waiting for him. The metalwork on the harnesses having been completed, he took a second and picked up a rag and wiped his brow, letting the red-hot horseshoe he had been working on cool in a bucket of water, the steam rising from the hissing sound it made.

He took out his pocket watch and looked at the time. It was 11:43 A.M., on the morning of June 7th.

Snapping shut the lid and putting the watch back in his pocket, the blacksmith stood in amazement as the anvil fell off its stand as the earth began to shake. Large cracks began to appear all around him and the sand became like liquid and started to slide toward the sea. He quickly grabbed on to one of the support beams of his shop, but everything was moving . . . sliding . . . and then with a sound like thunder, the earth came apart completely and the thatch roof of the shop caved in upon itself and slid into the sea and was gone.

Isaac, having only moved ten yards from the warehouse when it all began, stood frozen with fear as everything around him began to slide to the sea. Regaining his senses, he looked around and headed for the dock master's office only a few yards away, which had a second story so those in the office could see the ships coming in and out of the harbor. He entered and felt the building starting to move but headed up the steps to the second floor. He stared out the window and couldn't believe his eyes. Everything around him was sliding into the sea. He was amazed when he looked at the warehouse that had so intrigued him. It was standing fast even though all around it slid on a river of sand into the harbor, but there was no splash . . . no real sound at all other than the rumblings of the earth. He couldn't understand why the water hadn't risen into the air at the impact, but then he stared out at the sea and realized it was no longer near the shore. It was moving backward, away from the land.

His grandmother practiced black magic and had told him stories, and surely this must be the work of the Evil One. He almost fell as the building lurched forward, and he had to grab at a sliding desk to steady himself. Just as he looked up, he cried out. The water that had run away from Port Royal was coming back, rising to a height of over six feet, and Isaac did the only thing he could do. He closed his eyes and waited. His last memory being that of a giant wall of water crashing through the glass seconds before the dock master's office . . . that grand building . . . and Isaac . . . became one with that water, water that now covered the strange warehouse, its roof visible beneath the surface of the Caribbean Sea.

CHAPTER 3

January 1972

Sebastian Powell was busy cleaning up the mess. It had been one of those nights where the alcohol was running like water at Firefly, the estate of his employer, Noel Coward. With Peter O'Toole and Richard Burton present, it always seemed to end the same way, and tonight had been no exception. The drunken brawl had started early, and it had taken several servants to separate the combatants and send them to their rooms.

Sebastian chuckled to himself as he carried in another tray of dirty glasses to the bar. He looked around at the stone structure. He had heard the tales. The place had once been a lookout point for the famous Henry Morgan, and when Noel Coward bought the property and built his home, he converted the building into an outdoor bar, and Sebastian could only think it had seen more action than it had during the time of the famous pirate.

It was late, and he was just cleaning off the last of the brass coasters in Mr. Coward's set that had been given to him, supposedly, by Errol Flynn, one of his neighbors. It must have been because he was tired that the coaster slipped from his hand and fell behind the cabinet where he had been working. He pushed the cabinet away, barely getting it to move enough to reach the coaster. Once he had secured it, he went to move the cabinet back, when the overhead fluorescent lights caught something, an irregularity in the stone work, and he moved the cabinet further out to examine it. It looked like one of the stones was sitting on edge, with one ending touching the stone next to it, but a space was underneath the left portion of the stone and it jutted out just a fraction from the wall. Thinking it had come loose, Sebastian pressed the top of the stone on the left to see if he could force it down so it would touch and secure its position. But when he pushed the stone, grabbing it and pulling it slightly, the stone came free in his hand. He got up and went and got a flashlight and came back and looked in the hole left by the stone and saw a leather case.

Looking around to make sure no one else was there, he took the leather case out and set it on the counter and opened it. Inside were what appeared to be several writings, and when he touched one it began to crumble. Very carefully, he moved his hand over the rest in the leather pouch. He then noticed there was a folded piece of leather, which he carefully removed and opened, but he couldn't recognize what it was. The truth be told, Sebastian had never learned to read. It was one of the reasons he had the second job at Firefly, in addition to his day job of working in the fields. He was saving money so that if he ever had children, they would be able to get an education and not have to suffer the indignities he had of being unable to read.

He took his time and made sure the stone was put back as he had found it, stuck the leather folder in the back of his waistband, where it was covered by his waiter's jacket, and moved quickly to finish cleaning up.

Once everything was secured, he jumped on his moped that was parked next to the bar and headed down to Port Maria, knowing that he had found something important, although he wasn't quite sure what it was.

CHAPTER 4

Andre Powell was fifteen years old when his father, Sebastian Powell, was diagnosed with cancer and given only six months to live.

Andre watched his father weaken and wither away, but it wasn't until near the end when he was called to the small bedroom in the shack where he and his father lived in Port Maria.

"Andre, me be tough on yu. Me know nanna easy. When yu Mudda died when yu born, me naah know wa to do. I lef yu to be by yuself too much, a me to work. Andre, yu a smart boy. Yu do well in de school, yu read, a me proud yu. Me hab to tell yu somting important . . . somting dat could mek yu life."

He then directed Andre to an area on the wooden floor and told him to pry up a board that was loose. Andre found it and looked up at his father, almost beginning to cry as the light from the tiny lamp on the table made his sunken features look like a skull.

"Reach onda, boy," said Sebastian, "a pull out dat dere."

Andre did what he was told and pulled out a leather pouch and a burlap bag.

"Now bring dem dah to me, boy. Bring dem dah here," said Sebastian.

And again Andre did as he was told. Sebastian took the leather pouch and opened it. He showed Andre pieces of parchment inside.

"Yu hab be real careful, Andre. Papa be vedy brittle a fall apart if yu naah be careful. Me know dey important, but me naah know wa dey be. Yu got to find bassmon who unnerstan it a see wa dem dah mean. Den," said Sebastian, "dere be dis."

As he reached for it, he began to cough and his whole body began to shake, the cancer in his lungs taking hold of him, and Andre, who had been sitting on the side of the bed, stood up and put his hands on his father's shoulders, trying to keep him still.

Finally, the attack was over. Clearing his throat, Sebastian began again.

"Dere be dis, Andre. Me tink it be a map. Wa be say up dere?"

"It say 'Morgan's Map', Faada."

"Me tink dis. Me find dese dere at Firefly. Member when me took yu up dere a yu helped me stock de bar dat day? Bar used be a lookout fa de pirate, Henry Morgan."

Andre's eyes widened. He had heard the legends and the stories about Morgan all his life, and he had a love for the sea and pirates and adventure.

"Faada," said Andre, looking at the map, "cooyah! There be an X! Dis be de treasa map, Faada! Be de pirate treasa map! Start right her whe we hab de ouse in Port Maria and godeh down to Port Royal."

"Meebe, son," said Sebastian, forcing a smile, "or meebe it lead to somting naah so good. Yu got be careful, boy. Like me said, yu got find de right peoples a get dem look at dis a help yu."

He took Andre's hand and said, "Me mek sure yu be safe, Andre, after me a go. Naah going be easy, son. Yu can do it. Yu a man now. It be arright."

Andre felt the tears welling in his eyes and willed himself not to cry.

"Yu talk crazy, Faada. Yu be der de marrows. Yu naah gwine nahwhe."

Sebastian's face became stern as he squeezed Andre's hand.

"Listen, boy . . . me . . . me dying. Yu hab to come to grips wid dat a de fact dat me gonna go. Yu hab tek care of yu. Dis will help yu," and he handed Andre the burlap sack. "Go ahead . . . look in dere," said Sebastian, as Andre set the heavy sack beside him on the bed.

Reaching inside, Andre pulled out a handful of Jamaican dollars and British sterling and looked in amazement at his father.

"Me save all de life, Andre, to mek sure ma pickney hab somting. It be yours, boy. Me waan yu promise me yu git edicasion. Use dat dere money to git yu de good life."

Andre kept reaching into the bag and pulling out more and more coins, amazed at how many there were . . . more than any he'd ever seen in his entire life.

"Andre!" snapped Sebastian, "Promise me!"

Andre shook his head.

"Me promise, Faada. Me promise."

"Arright," said Sebastian, "now me tired. Put dat dere back in de hole a cover it up wid de floorboard. We talk more later."

Andre once again did as he was told, and after he had secured the items in the floor, he came over and kissed his father goodnight and went to sleep on his own small cot, but that sleep did not come easily with thoughts racing through his head . . . in conflict with sorrow because he knew his father was dying and wonder at what the future might hold given what he had just been shown.

The next talk between Andre and his father never came. Andre woke the next morning to find that his father was gone.

There was a whirlwind of relatives and friends coming to the small house in Port Maria and expressing their condolences. Even the Blackwell family that now was in charge of the Firefly Estate sent food and stopped by to make sure Andre was all right.

Sebastian Powell was buried in Port Maria Cemetery with his ancestors and after the appropriate period of mourning, Andre Powell found himself alone.

CHAPTER 5

Going into the house, Andre went into his father's bedroom and pried open the floorboard and took out the leather case. He set it on the floor and carefully took out the papers and tried to read what they said, but the writing was difficult to understand, and although he could make out certain words, he couldn't make out exactly what the papers were.

He took out the folded piece of leather and opened it and smiled. He put the parchment back in the leather pouch and put it back underneath the floorboard with the burlap bag full of money and made sure the floorboard was secure. He headed outside to find his best friend for as long as he could remember, Billy Lewis.

He found Billy in an alley, arguing with a man he did not know, whom Billy had pinned against a wall.

"Billy! Leave dat guy alone!" said Andre. "Me got somting better to show yu!"

"Anneda minute, Andre!" shot back Billy. "Dis ginnal (liar) owes us money . . . dat be tru?" he asked pointedly at the man, whose back was pressed up against the wall.

"Me told you, mon . . . me no hab dat right now. Me gitt it fa yu de marrows."

Billy looked at Andre and smiled and then patted the man on the back.

"De marrows, mon, or me agn find yu. Yu unnerstan?"

The man nodded. Billy walked toward Andre, smiling the whole way.

"Wa so Jessum Piece (special) yu got fa me, Andre?"

"Naah here," said Andre. "We go me ouse."

They went to Andre's house, where Andre had Billy wait outside while he retrieved the leather case and burlap sack. When he came out, Andre said, "We a go de cave."

They made their way along the shoreline to a secluded point where boulders jutted out from the hillside onto the beach and went behind several rocks to where they were obscured from view by anyone walking along the beach. They pushed aside the foliage to reveal the mouth of the cave. They went in and sat down on the rock outcropping, as they had done ever since they found this place as little children.

"Check yu dis," said Andre, "be de pirate treasa map." He showed Billy the map he had taken from the leather pouch. Billy looked at it, turning it various ways in his hand.

"Dut dere be no pirate map," he said.

"Hell it naah be," said Andre.

"Wa nah yu tink dat dis be de pirate map?" asked Billy.

"Right dere . . . see wa dis say?"

Billy flew into a rage and threw the piece of leather at Andre.

"You be fun of me, mon?" he asked.

"Be cool, brudda," said Andre. "Jist fooling a little. Here, me tell yu wa dis say," and he went over the map with Billy, who had never learned how to read. When he was done, Billy walked around the cavern with the map in his hand.

"Morgan, huh? He be a pirate. Hmmm. So if dis be right, dere be treasa down in de Port Royal?"

"Could be," said Andre, "me nanna know."

Billy looked out of the cave entrance, past the beach, at the sea, and then looked back at Andre.

"Dese words down here . . . wa de hell do dis mean?

"Me nanna know," said Andre. "Me a go find sombody to figure dis out.

Billy seemed irritated again and threw the piece of leather towards Andre. It landed on the floor of the cave.

"Hey," said Andre, "yu be easy! Yu ruin dis!"

"Me nanna ruining shit," said Billy. "Dat be nah pirate treasa map . . . jist be some fool bein' fun wid de stupid pickney."

Now it was Andre's turn to be irritated.

"Wa de hell do yu know?"

"Me tell yu wa me know 'bout dis," came a voice from the front of the cave, as Damian Henry entered. "Yu two be done wid de argie a be gaan to de work."

Not having heard their conversation, Damian asked, "Wa be de argie 'bout dat keep yu two be gaan de work?"

Andre quickly bent over and picked up the piece of leather, turned, folded it, and put it in his jeans pocket as Damian negotiated the entrance to the cave and walked toward them.

"Cooyah!" exclaimed Damian. "Wa be dis?" he said, picking up the leather case and the burlap sack.

"Dey be papas . . . me Faada lef me," said Andre, exchanging a look with Billy that told him not to say anything. Billy nodded.

Damian opened the burlap sack and smiled and then looked in the leather pouch, making sure there was nothing in it but papers. He threw the leather case at Andre.

"Dat be yurs." Pointing at the bag, he said, "Dis be fa me. Whole heap be fa me."

What Andre could never bring himself to tell his father was that at the age of thirteen he had become a member of the Shower Posse, the most feared drug cartel in Jamaica and worked as a collector in Port Maria and the surrounding towns. Billy had gone with him, and they did the collecting together, with Damian Henry as their boss.

Neither Billy nor Andre like Damian. He was cruel and vicious and enjoyed hurting people when they didn't have the money to pay for the drugs. He and Billy always tried to do what they could for people, understanding their situation and giving them time whenever possible to make good on what they owed, but far too often Damian would step in, seemingly for the sheer pleasure of it, and break bones or worse until payment was obtained. He considered Andre and Billy soft.

There was no reasoning with Damian and too often Andre and Billy were sickened by what they were ordered to do in collecting money from their own poor neighbors and people they knew . . . but Damian was a boss, and they had no choice . . . but what he was trying to do right now, taking away the only thing that Andre's father left him, was something Andre could not let go.

"Wadda yu mean brudda? Dose Jamaicans belong to me. Me Faada gave dem to me befo he died. Dey be fa me future."

Damian smiled, walked up to Andre, and put his hand around his shoulders.

"Don't be dum, mon. Be smart. Me be de future. Whe a go, yu go. Yu see?"

"But Damian . . ." began Andre.

Damian put his finger to his lips and squeezed Andre's shoulders harder than necessary.

"We say dis be fa yu a Billy dere bein late alla time."

He looked at Billy.

"Now, me axe yu . . . dat be nah fair?"

Billy put his head down. Damian raised his voice.

"Me axe yu, Billy!"

Billy looked at Andre and Andre nodded.

"Sure, Damian. Dat be fair."

Damian looked at Andre.

"See? Yu brudda . . . he know it be fair. Now, yu two pickneys best be to work, a de money best be comin' to Damian."

"Yes, bassmon," said Andre, gritting his teeth, as he and Billy headed for the exit of the cave.

"Anneda ting," said Damian, stopping them before they left, "nahbody be late no more. De payments dey be on time . . . or dat dere trouble begin."

And with that, Damian brushed by them, exited the cave, and was gone.

"Sorry, brudda," said Billy. "Dat shit naah right."

"Me know," said Andre. "Dat 'enry be one gravalishus (greedy) ginnal. He mek de big mistake dis time," said Andre. "Som day he pay."

Billy slapped Andre one the shoulder. "Meebe yu be right, but dat be som day. Dis day we gotta be to dah work. Shit!" continued Billy. "Som day meebe we hunt fa dat dere pirate treasa be in yur pocket," and they both started laughing as they headed out to begin their collections.

CHAPTER 6

Several years later, Professor Wesley Dixon was eating breakfast when he noticed a young man across from him reading a copy of the Jamaica Gleaner.

"Any important news?"

The young man looked up from the paper and seemed to be studying him when he replied, "Nah, mon. Be the same old shit."

"Ah," said the Professor. "That's too bad. I was hoping there was something we would be able to discuss over breakfast."

"Naah likely, bassmon. Yu be deh edicasion . . . me, nah."

The Professor laughed.

"Well, you're reading the paper, so obviously, you're interested."

Andre Powell turned the paper so the Professor could see.

"Gotta check de odds, mon. Me gotta talk later wid dem dat lose der bets."

The Professor lowered his head.

"I see."

Realizing that the young man was part of one of the many criminal syndicates on the island and that, discretion being the better part of valor, he should cease the conversation.

Andre got up and threw some Jamaicans on the table for his bill and walked past Professor Dixon. He turned and looked back.

"Yu be a teacha?" asked Andre.

"Yes," said the Professor.

"Whe?" asked Andre.

"I travel to many places. I try and teach the culture of Jamaica to different people. In a few weeks, I'll be going to England."

"Cooyah!" said Andre. "Across de sea?"

"Yes," laughed the Professor, "across the sea."

"Wa be de interest of de people dere?" asked Andre.

"I'm giving a seminar, a course, on Captain Henry Morgan. He was originally from the British Isles, and they have great interest in him and others like him and their history in this area. That's sort of my specialty."

"Morgan, eh?" said Andre. "De pirate?"

"Well, actually, he was a private . . ." and he stopped in mid-sentence. "Yes," the Professor smiled, "the pirate."

Andre thought for a while, rubbing his chin.

"Yu be here evy day?"

"Yes, I eat breakfast here practically every morning."

"Meebe me bring yu somting," said Andre. "Me check yu later."

And with that, he walked down the steps and was gone.

The Professor thought to himself, "What could you bring to me, young man, that I might be interested in?" He shook his head, but he also knew that sometimes very important things came from very strange places.

This was proven true two weeks later. The Professor arrived for his usual breakfast, and there was a leather pouch waiting for him.

"Where'd this come from?" the Professor asked the waiter.

"Dat kid yu be talking wid . . . couple week ago . . . he lef it here fa yu."

"I see," said the Professor. "Well, thank you."

"Yah, mon," said the waiter.

It was not long before Professor Wesley Dixon's breakfast was sitting in front of him, cold, as, with amazement, he carefully read page after page of the documents contained in the leather pouch and realized what a treasure he had just received.

PRESENT DAY

CHAPTER 7

It was all out warfare on the streets of Kingston as the Jamaican military and police invaded that section of Kingston that belonged to the Shower Posse, searching for the Posse's leader and one of the world's major drug lords, Christopher "Dudus" Coke, trying to fill an extradition request from the United States.

For two days in May 2010, Tivoli Gardens was a war zone with over seventy-three civilians killed and thirty-five wounded. Four members of the military and police were also killed and five hundred arrests were made as battles waged in the Gardens.

Coke was captured and extradited to the United States to spend the rest of his life in prison.

In the vacuum after his departure, the more ruthless and cunning members of the Posse went to war amongst themselves to become the leader. And when it all ended, that one was Damian Henry. As he consolidated his power, he brought Andre Powell with him to Kingston and made him one of his lieutenants, placing him in charge of the whole northern coast for collections, distribution, and enforcement.

Now Billy worked for Andre, and, together, they had prospered and had become well known for the lack of violence they used in settling disputes and collecting debts for the cartel.

Andre was no saint. He had hurt people, and he had killed people when necessary, but he took no pleasure in it, and it was always the last resort. He had no delusions. He knew he was a criminal, and a criminal high in the ranks of one of the most evil and vicious drug cartels in the world.

He thought of his father, and his only hope was that someday he would get to that better place where his father wanted him to go. These thoughts swam through Andre's head as he drove down the A3 from Port Maria to Kingston.

Damian had called a special meeting, announcing there was extremely important news he had to give to his lieutenants, and he had let it be known that they would be spending their time on a new mission for the cartel.

When Andre arrived at Damian's secret retreat off the A4 in Easington, he was the last of the lieutenants to enter. The rest were seated around a table in a modern equipped conference room, and Damian rose as he came in.

"Now we be startin'," he said. "De bassmon hab arrive."

He walked up to Damian and hugged him.

"Me brudda!" he said. "Evyting arright?"

"Yah, why? It be good," said Andre.

"Good!" said Damian, shaking his hand. "Sit . . . ovr dere . . . sit . . . we be start."

Damian paced back and forth in front of the lieutenants.

"Opportunity, opportunity," he said. "It be here. Dose crazy Arabs, de ISIS. Dey tek dose fields in Afghanistan . . . de poppy fields . . . dey own dem now. Dey pickin one mon to be de mon do de distributin' of all de heroin from dose fields to de north . . . a dey here in Jamaica . . . a de one dey waan be me. Yu axe why me wanna deal wid dem? We be, if dis work, de biggest cartel. We expand dere . . . a dere . . . a dere," he said, pointing to a map on the wall, "all ovr

de Caribbean . . . a we control supply dere," he said, pointing to the
United States.

"Why?"

"So we be rich!" he said laughing.

The lieutenants all joined in laughing with him, even Andre,
but it was Andre who asked, "Wa be de catch?"

Smiling, Damian moved toward Andre, pointing his finger at
him.

"See? Dis . . . he be de tinker. De catch be five hundred million
U.S. dollah!"

One of the lieutenants whistled.

"See?" said Damian. "See wa he tink? We canna do dis. Dat
is why yu be here. Yu four . . . yu be tinkin' how we can get dese
monies, soon. Dis deal be soon. Me no care who or how. We kill.
We steal. We do whateva dis tek so dem-deh poppies be ours. Go
find de money," and he turned and walked out of the room.

"Five hundred mil," said one lieutenant. "Dat big numba."

"Shit!" said one of the other ones, "Dere be no way. Dem kinda
numbas from dis island? No mon . . . no way."

"Wa say yu, Andre?" asked one of the lieutenants. "Dere be a
way?"

Andre was deep in thought, wondering if perhaps . . . nah, it
was only a legend.

"Nah," said Andre. "Me got no idea, but me know dis . . . 'cause
me know him . . . we be better com up wid somting."

CHAPTER 8

It was two weeks later when Andre was going up the steps to the balcony of the Casa Marie Hotel to read the paper and have a cup of Blue Mountain coffee. The brainstorming of the lieutenants had not brought any great success in developing a plan to obtain half a billion dollars in a short period of time. They had learned that their window was a month's time, and it appeared to be an impossible task.

Andre had thought about bringing Billy in to see what he could come up with, but Billy wasn't a dreamer of big ideas, he was satisfied collecting and running ganga, coke, and heroin. He had three little kids now, and he and his wife, Maria, were deeply in love.

Andre was happy for Billy and yearned for his simple life, but knew that it was not going to be. He was in too deep, and he couldn't think of a way to get out.

When he got to the balcony, three or four of the waiters were looking at the morning edition of the newspaper. They stopped as Andre approached, and one showed him to his table.

"Wa so big in deh papa?" he asked, and his waiter brought him a copy of the morning edition, along with his cup of coffee. The coffee remained untouched as Andre, startled, read the headlines, "Captain Morgan a Traitor". He quickly read the story.

"Deh teacha," he said to himself, when he saw that the story had been written about a paper Dr. Wesley Dixon had presented in London, based upon documents he had received the previous year from a Jamaican, detailing Morgan's plans to create a Spanish governorship for the entire Caribbean. And then came the part of the story that made Andre's blood run cold, even on that hot, sunny morning. The story went on to say that Professor Dixon had received the papers from a young man from Port Maria named Andre Powell, and that, according to the papers, there was a treasure map showing the location of the lost Incan treasures from Morgan's raid on Panama that had been lost for centuries . . . believed to have a value in excess of one-half billion dollars . . . and that the treasure map was not with the papers he had been given.

"Shit!" said Andre, as he threw down a few Jamaicans and ran down the steps, heading for his car.

THE PIRATE MAP

CHAPTER 9

Damian Henry was reading the same article at his secret hideaway in Easington. After he completed the article, he calmly finished his breakfast and then walked out onto the balcony. Overlooking the grounds, he thought to himself, "Andre . . . Andre," and he shook his head. "Yu be de ginnal," thought Damian. "Yu deceive me, boy. Yu hab de treasa map. Yu hab de way to wa me need . . . de money. Sorry, mon . . . yu gonna pay fa dis."

Then he turned and asked one of the staff for another cup of coffee.

Andre was en route to Port Antonio, driving along A4, the coast road, trying to figure out what he was going to do. Pounding the steering wheel, he said out loud, "He know. He know me got de map. Dat dere treasa be jist wa he need. He be a crazy mon. Me canna go dere. Me canna esplain. He tink me keep fa me. He gonna kill me dead."

Just then his cell phone rang, and he almost swerved off the road at the shock of the sound. He hit the button on his phone.

"Who dis?"

"Who yu tink, Andre?" said Damian. "How my brudda today?"

"Me be fine, Damian. Me be fine."

"Good. Me need yu com to me ouse. Me be tinkin' of a new plan, but me need yu help to mek dis work."

"Sure, Damian. Me be dere, but naah til de marrows."

"Me see," said Damian. "De marrows, den. Meebe me tink of anneda way by den. Me work on somting dis night, a den me let yu know."

"Arright," said Andre, and then he hung up. "Dat's it," thought Andre, "me got tonight to get out. De marrows, me be dead."

CHAPTER 10

Andre had driven along the Coast Highway for several hours planning an escape so he could avoid certain death at the hands of Damian Henry. He had turned inland at Port Antonio and gone upward into the Blue Mountains to Windsor, where he pulled off in a secluded clearing with a view of the lush green valleys around him and began to formulate a plan.

Getting out of his Range Rover, one of the perks he enjoyed as a lieutenant in the Shower Possee, he sat on a flat rock and gazed out over the green forest, a waterfall cascading into the valley on his right, that eventually fed into the Rio Grande.

"Me canna belief dis," he thought. "De dere map Billy a me joke 'bout as pickneys be real. Dere be de treasa at Port Royal an de map hold de key to findin' it."

Andre had called Billy on his cell phone several times after speaking with Damian and had no success in reaching him. As he sat and thought, he came to a conclusion.

"De map be de key to it all," he thought. "Ebbybody be waan' it ... Damian, de Arab bastards, a de Americans."

He thought back to a meeting that he had attended in Tivoli Gardens. Damian had introduced an "American businessman" who had come to Jamaica to indicate his government's concern for certain Arab interests trying to take over his businesses on the island and asked for the cartel's help in protecting those interests. When the meeting was over, Damian had spoken with Andre.

"De Americans be ginnals. Dey talk both sides of de mouth. Dat bastard in Miami, Jake Sullivan, put me boys away evy chance he git, a dis bastard com down a beg me help agin de Arabs. De business dat mon be in be CIA. It de government dat waan our help, Andre. Wa yu tink of dat?"

"Dey gonna stop goin' afta our boys?" asked Andre.

"He say dat be part of de deal, but who know. Me don trust de American bastards any more me do de Arab ones. Me got de big plans fa us, Andre. Me mek de deal wid de Arabs. We gonna own it all. De Americans . . . dey give me nuttin' me no arredy got. Me no fraid de Americans. Me time comin'. Me tek out dis Jake Sullivan a be done wid him. Den dey see who be fraid of who."

Everyone in the cartel had heard of Jake Sullivan. Since South Florida was such an entry point for its drug running in the United States and he was the Chief Federal Prosecutor for the area, he was the one who went after the cartel members and put a significant number in prison. They also knew of his exploits and that he was not a man to be trifled with. It was funny, but it was his close relationship with the President of the United States that had kept him alive – the fear being that taking him out would lead to severe reprisals against the Posse.

"Damian, he go mek de move now doh," thought Andre. "He hab de Arab bastards do it fa him. Be anneda terror shot at de U.S. . . . . an naah de Posse doin," and that's when Andre made his decision.

"Me be gwine back Port Maria . . . get de map a ed fa de boat a sail to de U.S. . . . . me axe fa de Jake Sullivan a negotiate de map wid de bassmon fa me freedom. Me savin' his ass . . . de mon be tankful a me be free . . . a mebbe Sullivan go afta Damian a de Arab bastards a me tek deh hol ting."

Standing up, he jumped down from the rock and headed for the Range Rover, feeling much better that he had made a decision. Now, if only he could contact Billy.

He had just started to laugh, thinking about Billy and him fighting over the map in the cave and Billy being adamant the map was a fake, when he had a horrible thought. He remembered his conversation with Damian and thought to himself, "Damian say he be trying anneda way to git wa he waan from me tonight. He be in de cave dat day. He know Billy know 'bout de map. Shit!" thought Andre. "Me brudda naah know . . . he naah know whe de map may be . . . me neba tell him. Me a go his ouse right now."

Realizing Damian's plan and Billy's vulnerability, he ran to the Range Rover, threw it in gear, and sped down the road toward the A4 and Port Antonio, where he would turn left and drive along the coast to Port Maria, praying that he could get there in time.

CHAPTER 11

It was 10:00 P.M. by the time Andre arrived at Port Maria. He had ditched his Range Rover in Golden Grove and took one of the many vehicles he had stored in various places along the northern coast to use in his drug running and collections, always trying to stay one step ahead of the Jamaican Constabulary Force and their narcotics division.

He parked on the outskirts of town and made his way to his house. Moving around the outside and making sure no one was there, he entered and found what he thought he would. The interior had been thoroughly searched – table and chairs upturned, cushions sliced, cabinet doors opened, broken items on the floor, and a loose floorboard where his father had kept his treasa, lifted and cast aside.

"Mebbe," he thought to himself, "dey com here a go. Now dey hunt fa me. Dat be good . . . dey naah catch me."

But the dread in his gut wouldn't go away. He knew Damian, and he knew exactly what he would do. Even if it might not get him what he wanted, he would take pleasure in the doing of it, and he headed to Billy's house, having called several times while on the road and still getting no answer.

When he arrived, he went through the same routine, coming to the house from a back alley and searching all the streets in the area to make sure there were no members of the cartel lying in wait.

"Dey be gone," he thought. "Dey a go Port Antonio whe me say me be. Dey be lookin' fa me. Afta dey be at me ouse, dey go."

Andre was trying to convince himself, and a small amount of hope was replacing some of the dread he felt, but that hope left as soon as he opened the door and walked into Billy's house.

He had to put his hand over his mouth to stifle the horrible scream that started in the pit of his stomach and rose through his throat as he fell to his knees. Lowering his head almost to the floor, he began to sob.

"Nah! Nah! Billy! Nah . . . naah dis! Naah dis!" and he pounded his hand on the floor in rage.

After several minutes he got up and made his way to the chair where Billy sat, bound and gagged. He had been tortured . . . beaten almost beyond recognition, and the ends of the fingers of each hand had been cut off. Andre, through his tears, could barely bring himself to look at Billy, but he did, and he put his hand on his face.

"Ah, Billy . . . me sorry. Dis be me fault."

Then he looked down at Billy's feet, where each of his three children lay, blood coming from the bullet holes in the backs of their heads, and next to him his wife, her clothes in disarray, shot in the same way . . . but Andre knew, only after horrible things had been done to her by the men who had been here.

Andre went and sat upright a chair that had been tossed on its side and sat down, looking at the scene.

"Dey start wid de beatin', like always," he thought. "But Billy, he can naah gim dem wa dey waan."

He closed his eyes, imagining the pain his friend had endured.

"Den dey go to de fingers . . . one by one . . . a he still naah tell dem. Den his wife. Den de pickneys . . . a still he naah tell dem. Den dey put de bullet in de ead."

He had seen it before. He'd even participated in tortures. He'd administered the kill shot . . . "But dis," he thought, "neba dis. Naah deh wife . . . de pickneys . . . me nah animal. Nah, nah . . . neba . . . neba dis."

He sat there looking at his friend and slaughtered family and knew he was done with the Shower Posse . . . that he was done with Damian. But if he was going to avenge Billy, he had to move.

He went to the back room of the house, pulled out the floorboard he had prepared one day when Billy and his family were gone, and reached into the small space he had created, pulled out an oilskin, opened it, and took out a piece of leather, looked at it, wrapped it back up in the oilskin, and put it in his pocket. He had never told Billy about it, so Billy could never tell his killers where the map was.

"He be tellin' de trut," Andre thought. "De poor bastard. He hab no chance," and he went back and stood by Billy. "Dis be me fault, brudda. Me mek de promise. Me tek care of dem dat did dese, a me com back anneda day, a me tek care of yu a de wife a pickneys, proper. Me go U.S., but me com back. Damian mek de big mistake . . . he gonna pay fa it . . ." and Andre Powell patted the cheek of his lifelong friend Billy, and thinking of nothing but revenge, walked out of the small shack in Port Maria into the night.

CHAPTER 12

Andre made his way through the alleys and shadows, never moving in a direct line to his destination – the boat slips at Port Maria. It took more time, but he believed that the killers from the cartel were looking for him elsewhere, never believing he would have come back to his home. Still, he was careful and looked all around him as he made his way down the ramp to where his boat was anchored. It had been bought under an assumed name, and actually was one of several he had berthed along the north shore, never knowing when he would have to run from the authorities.

He laughed to himself as he threw off the lines and started the engine as quietly as he could.

"De blood oath . . . shit! De Posse members . . . dey kill each udder all de time. Damian . . . he like de blood too much. Dere be no second chances wid Damian. Yu fuck up . . . yu be dead. A now, it be me turn. But de bastards, dey naah gonna git me . . . me a go git dem."

The boat was kept stocked with all the provisions, weapons, charts and anything else he might need, and he headed out to the Windward Passage, checking the charts and his GPS, setting a course that would take him as close as he could to the southeast tip of Cuba. Passing between it and Hispaniola, he would then curl around the island and head in a northwest direction for the

Florida Keys. He estimated landfall to be sometime mid-morning and knew he would have a long night ahead of him.

When he was a few miles off shore, the lights of Port Maria starting to dim, he throttled the engine full speed and continued to scan the horizon and look and listen for any signs of pursuit. So far, there were none. As he moved farther away, the coastline of Jamaica began to recede, and he wondered if and when he would come back.

"Nah . . . me be back," he thought. "Me promise Billy, an me promise Damian 'enry, so me be back."

His passage was uneventful. The waters were calm, and the wind was only a slight breeze. The boat's small cabin down below was fitted out with a microwave, getting power from the boat's generator, and he warmed up several mugs of his favorite Blue Mountain coffee and drank them through the night to keep him awake and alert, not that he could have slept had he wanted to. His feelings of remorse and anger stirred his mind, along with thoughts of his unknown future.

CHAPTER 13

The sun rose on a beautiful day as Andre entered the Florida Straits. Andre knew the Florida current, at the beginning of the Gulf Stream, exiting from the Gulf of Mexico, would want to push him northward, but he kept his engines on full throttle, and using his GPS, set a course to make landfall just north of Key West, at the narrowest point between the United States and Cuba, where the Straits were only about ninety-three miles wide.

It wasn't long before he made out land on the horizon and again checked behind him as he had continuously done throughout the voyage, and still saw no one coming after him.

"Look like me be to de U.S.A.," he said to himself, as the landform in front of him began to take shape.

As the coastline came into view, he cut back his engines and slowed, knowing that the boat was going to run aground, but he was unconcerned, knowing he wouldn't be using it again.

So it was at approximately 11:00 A.M., when Andre Powell ran ashore on Boca Chica Key, just as he had planned. He jumped out of the boat into the water and made his way up the beach to an expansive, neatly manicured lawn, when a heavy-set, red-faced man in a floral shirt, shorts, and flip-flops came barreling out of his lanai, pointing a shotgun at him and screaming.

"Stop right there, you son-of-a-bitch! Who the hell do you people think you are that you can just come into this country? Pull up a Goddamn boat right on my lawn! Who the hell do you think you are?"

He leveled the weapon at Andre.

"Better start talking to me, boy!"

Never taking his eyes off the man or his shotgun, Andre slowly sank to his knees on the cool, green grass, and intertwined his fingers behind his head.

"Me talk de Jake Sullivan."

"The hell you say!" said the man. "Jake Sullivan, my ass! I'm not going to ask you again. What are you doing here?"

But Andre would not respond. Just then the lanai door opened and out came a woman dressed in similar fashion to the man.

"Earl, what are you doing out . . . oh my God! Who's that?"

"That, Ruthie, is a Goddamn Rastafarian immigrant. Son-of-a-bitch pulled his boat right up on our lawn! Says he wants to talk to Jake Sullivan."

"Jake Sullivan?"

"Go in the house, Ruthie, and call the Sheriff's Department. I'm going to keep my eye on this one 'til they get here."

"Earl, don't do anything stupid."

"Ruthie, just go call the Sheriff. I'm taking care of this. Don't you move, now," said Earl, again pointing the shotgun at Andre.

Andre kept his eyes fixed on the grass in front of him but couldn't help thinking to himself, "Dese be crazy American bastards!"

CHAPTER 14

Only fifteen minutes after she had placed the call, a Monroe County Sheriff's vehicle, lights flashing, came to a screeching stop at the home of Earl and Ruth Fineman. Sheriff's Deputy Joshua Tate and his partner, Deputy Alfie Jones, exited the vehicle and walked through a gate on the side of the house, past the lanai to the back yard, as Ruthie had directed them. The noise of their entry made Earl turn his head away from Andre, but he never lowered the shotgun.

"It's about time you boys got here," he said. "I've been standing out in this hot sun keeping guard over this son-of-a-bitch this whole time."

"We're here now, Mr. Fineman," said Deputy Sheriff Tate. "You can lower the weapon, now, sir."

"What? Oh . . . yeah . . . all right." As he did so, he pointed at Andre. "Don't you be gettin' no ideas now, you understand? Come on, Ruthie. Let these boys take care of this. I need a drink," he said, as he pushed past the Deputies and Ruthie to enter the lanai.

"Now, Earl," said Ruthie, "you know it's too early in the morning for you to start."

"Ruthie, Goddamn it! There's a son-of-a-bitch Rastafarian in my back yard whose boat's parked out on my beach, and I got Sheriff's Deputies! I'll have a Goddamn drink if I want one!"

And with that, he slammed the door and went inside.

The two Sheriff's Deputies looked at each other and smiled, shaking their heads at the antics of Earl Fineman and his wife, and then they turned to the matter at hand and approached Andre, who was still kneeling, his eyes still focused on the grass in front of him.

"You go ahead and talk to him, Alfie," said Josh.

"Why? Because I'm black?" said Alfie.

"No . . . come on . . . nothing like that. Maybe he'll warm up to you."

"You are still such a cracker, Josh," said Alfie, shaking his head. "Sir," said Alfie, "can you tell us who you are and why you're here?"

Andre was silent and his gaze remained locked in front of him.

"Sir, we can't help you if you aren't willing to help us. Do you understand what I'm asking you?"

Andre raised his head and looked at the Sheriff's Deputies.

"Me unnerstan, but yu gotta unnerstan. Me talk to de Jake Sullivan. Dat be all me say. Dis de way it hab to be."

"Let me get this straight," said Deputy Sheriff Tate. "You want to talk to Jake Sullivan, the Federal Prosecutor in Miami? And you're not going to say anything else?"

Andre looked up again. "Dat be it," and resumed staring at the grass.

Josh motioned Alfie to move back with him toward the house, where they spoke in a hushed whisper.

"I don't know what's with this guy, but he's crazy. Jake Sullivan, my ass."

"Yeah, but what are we going to do with him?"

"I'll tell you what we're going to do. I'm calling the Naval Air Station. This guy, who I guess came from Jamaica, made illegal entry into the United States. This is a federal immigration problem. I'm calling the Naval Air Station. Let them take care of it. You stay here and watch him. I'll go to the car and phone it in."

"All right, man," said Alfie. "Sounds good to me. I think this is a problem we don't need."

"Exactly," said Deputy Sheriff Tate, as he headed back down past the lanai, through the gate, and out to the car. Several minutes later, he came back.

"Anything going on?" he said. "He say anything?"

"Hasn't even moved," said Deputy Sheriff Jones.

"They said two NCIS Agents will be on their way. As soon as they get here, we're outta here. It doesn't matter if he says anything or not."

Soon, Earl came out, glass in hand.

"So, what's going on? You getting' this son-of-a-bitch off my lawn, or what?"

"We're taking care of things, Mr. Fineman, don't worry," said Sheriff's Deputy Tate. "We called the Naval Air Station. They're sending two agents out to pick him up and take him in."

"'Bout Goddamn time!" said Earl, walking back through the lanai door. "I can't believe that son-of-a-bitch just came up on my lawn . . . just like he owned the place."

And with that, the door slammed behind him.

CHAPTER 15

Agents Thomas Hood and Melissa Parker of the Naval Air Station in Key West, Boca Chica Field, arrived in less than ten minutes and entered the back of the house by the same route as the Sheriff's Deputies.

After discussing the situation, the Deputies turned over the situation to the two agents from NCIS and were on their way.

Agent Parker approached Andre, while her partner stood back, ready to draw his weapon, if necessary, and said, "Sir, I need you to get up and come with us."

Andre raised his face and stared at her.

"Me talk to de Jake Sullivan. Dat be it."

"Sir, we can't make this decision with you here. You need to come with us, and then we'll see what we can do."

Andre thought about this for a minute and then shook his head in the affirmative.

"All right, sir, first thing I need you to do is get up and put your hands behind your back."

Andre did as directed and Agent Parker put a set of plastic cuffs on his wrists.

"Now we're going to take you to our car, Mr. . . . . I didn't get your name."

Andre looked at her and smiled.

"Me no give yu de name. Me talk to de Jake Sullivan. Dat be it."

Agent Hood then took Andre's other arm and the two escorted him alongside the house and through the gate to their car. They put him into the back seat, pushing his head down to make sure he didn't hit it, got in, and headed for the Naval Air Station.

En route, they called in to have a team come impound the boat and bring it in to be searched for contraband.

Upon their arrival, they escorted Andre into a holding room and had him sit.

"Anything we can get you to eat or drink?" asked Agent Parker.

Andre looked at her.

"Me talk to de Jake Sullivan. Dat be it."

"All right, sir. Have it your way," and she exited. She went to her partner, who was looking through the glass window.

"Well, Melissa, what do you think?"

"He's got no I.D. . . . nothing."

"Boat the whole way from Jamaica?"

"Could be. Straits were quiet last night. Clear. Light wind. That boat he had on shore, which we have impounded, certainly seemed seaworthy. If he knew the waters, he could have made the run last night."

"They doing a search?"

"As we speak."

"Well, the dreadlocks and the cap are certainly Rastafarian."

"It would seem so," said Melissa. "And it would seem that's all we got. So, what do you want to do?"

"Agent Hood thought about it. I'm making a command decision, Melissa. I'm going to call Jake Sullivan, but first I'm going to talk to our friend in there," and he opened the door and entered the holding room.

"All right, sir. I'm in charge of this little situation we have here, and I will agree to place a call to Mr. Sullivan to see if he will speak with you as you wish. But I'm going to tell you that he will not speak with you unless you give me some information about who you are and why you're here. You give me that, and I'll make the call. Otherwise, we'll just put you in a holding cell until we can figure out what to do with you."

Andre thought. He knew he was safe here. First, the cartel didn't know he was here, and second, it was a Naval Air Station. Andre looked up.

"Okay, mon. Me name be Andre Powell. Me from Jamaica, and me be lieutenant in de Shower Posse. Me need be tellin' Sullivan 'bout de treasa waitin' in Jamaica . . . five hundred million dollah be de treasa. And de Posse waan it. De bastard Arabs waan it. Hell, mon, me even tink yu CIA be wantin' it. Big shit 'bout to happen, mon . . . and me, me know all 'bout it."

Agent Hood exited the holding room and looked at Agent Parker.

"Well, what do you think of that?"

"I'm thinking no one would be crazy enough to make up a story like that and then want to talk about it with Jake Sullivan. There's something going on."

"My thoughts exactly. I'm making the call."

And with that, he headed out to call Jake Sullivan.

Agent Hood had to explain the situation twice to Mr. Sullivan's secretary, and she came back on the line and said he and his investigator, Mike Lang, were on their way.

After receiving the information, Agent Hood reentered the holding room.

"Well, Mr. Powell, you got what you wanted. Jake Sullivan is on his way here to talk to you."

"Dat be good," said Andre, shaking his head. "Now, me tek up dat pretty lady's offer. Me would like somting to eat a drink while me wait fa de Jake Sullivan."

CHAPTER 16

"I know it sounds crazy, Les," said Jake as he spoke to the Attorney General of the United States, Lester Kirkland, "but that's what they're telling us."

"There's a lot going on with that cartel right now, that I can't get into, Jake, but if someone's talking about the Shower Posse and Arabs and a potential of a five hundred million dollar treasure, we need to look into it. I'll arrange for one of the Agency's jets to be ready to go at Miami International. You can take it down to Boca Chica. Call me as soon as you learn anything."

"All right, Les. Thanks," said Jake.

"What's up?" asked Mike Lang, Jake's chief investigator and best friend.

"I don't know, Mike. Something's going on. Les wouldn't say, but I get the feeling that this guy we're about to meet is somehow in play."

"Naturally, what would a day in the Keys be without government intrigue."

"It's not so bad," said Jake, "at least we get the jet . . . we don't have to drive."

"I don't know, Jake. Anytime those guys in Washington are being nice to us, it always seems to lead to problems."

With that, Jake got up and grabbed his "go" bag. Mike was already set to go.

"Well," said Jake, "let's go find out."

And they left the office and headed for the airport.

CHAPTER 17

In less than an hour, they touched down on one of the three runways at the Naval Air Station in Key West. Exiting the plane, they were met by Agents Parker and Hood, who brought them up to date on Andre Powell.

"All he initially kept saying was he wanted to talk to you. That's all he would say. Finally, I made him understand that you weren't coming to talk with him unless he gave us some information, and that's when he supplied me with the information I gave your secretary."

"Anything since then?" asked Mike.

"Just requested something to eat and drink, which we gave him. Other than that, he hasn't said a word."

"Well, let's go see the man," said Jake, "and find out what he wants to tell me."

The agents escorted Jake and Mike to the holding room and opened the door.

"Mr. Powell," said Agent Hood, "I'd like to introduce you to Jake Sullivan and his investigator, Mike Lang."

"Cooyah!" said Andre. "It be de mon . . . de Jake Sullivan . . . a de sidekick com, too."

"See," said Mike, "I keep telling you about this. Everybody thinks I'm your sidekick."

"We'll discuss it later," said Jake. "All right," said Jake, pulling up a chair and sitting down. "I'm here. What do you want to talk about?"

Just then, the door opened and a handsome black man standing six foot, three, probably in his early fifties, and obviously very fit, entered the room.

"Sorry to interrupt, Mr. Sullivan . . . Mr. Lang . . . Mr. Powell, but I wondered if I might be able to sit in?"

"Who the hell are you?" asked Mike.

A smile spread across the tall man's face as he extended his hand to Mike.

"My name is Mack Owens. Nice to meet you, Mr. Lang."

"Holy shit!" said Mike. "The Mack Owens?"

"Afraid so," said the tall man.

Mike sprung to his feet and quickly shook the tall man's hand.

"Pleasure's all mine, sir. Heard so much about you. Can't believe I'm meeting you in the flesh."

"Don't believe everything you hear, son."

Meanwhile, Jake was sitting there looking at the scene before him, a questioning look on his face that Mack Owens quickly recognized.

"Sorry, it appears that Mr. Sullivan here needs a brief update on who I am," and he extended his hand to Jake. "As I said, my name is Mack Owens. I'm an agent with the DEA."

"Bullshit!" said Andre Powell. "Dat mon be de Devil! We hunt yu fa years, mon, but yu de Devil . . . yu can naah die. Yu kill many of me friends, mon."

"You've killed many of mine, Mr. Powell," said Owens, his voice now cold. "Plus all the innocents, with your murder, mayhem, and drugs. It'll be my pleasure to put you away."

Andre smiled. "Me don tink so, mon. Me tell yu wa, mon . . me walk outta here de free mon. Yu like bet?"

"What kind of deal have you two made with this animal?"

"Hold on," said Jake. "Nobody's made any deals. Now let's go back to who you are, other than a DEA agent. What's the story, Mike?"

"Sorry, Mr. Owens. Jake, this man is a legend. He's a ghost. He's busted more cartels and put away more major drug dealers than anyone. There've been contracts on his life, like this asshole is talking about, since he became an agent. There've been more attempts on his life than you can count. He's honest to a fault. He always gets the guy he's going after. And, apparently, he's invincible."

"Hardly," laughed Mack. "Just lucky. But listen, you two have stories of your own, you know. I've heard about your exploits, too."

"Again," said Jake, "don't believe everything you hear."

"Are we ready now?" asked Mack, extending his hand again.

Jake smiled and stood up. "Nice to meet you. If Mike vouches for you, you're okay with me."

"That's good to know. Now, what's going on with Mr. Powell here?"

"All right, Andre. Tell this gentleman the story, too."

"Me naah be talkin' to dat son-of-a-bitch," said Andre.

"Look," said Jake, "you asked for this meeting. I'm about ready to get up and walk out that door unless you start talking. We all represent the United States Government, and that's who you're dealing with. So, I don't know what information you think you have that's going to let you walk out of here, but it's not going to happen. So, now's the time. Start talking, or I'm gone."

Andre shook his head in disgust, staring at Mack Owens. He pushed his chair back and then looked off into space.

"Have it your way," said Jake, and he stood up and headed for the door. His hand was on the handle when Andre spoke up.

"Arright, mon. Arright. Be cool. Be cool. Yu gotta git me yu word dat dere mon, he nah tek control of me. Yu two keep me safe.

Dat DEA he talk 'bout . . . dat full people from de Shower Posse, mon. We pay dem like pickneys eatin' candy."

"If that's true," said Owens, "there will be no deals unless you give me a list of who those people are."

"Me nah mek de deal wid yu, mon. Me mek de deal wid dem."

"Part of the deal," said Jake, "is to give him what he wants."

"Ah, bassmon, yu mek dis hard on poor Andre. Me com here to help, a yu do dis to me."

"Take it or leave it," said Jake.

"Arright . . . arright. Me gib yu all de information me got."

"Now, what's the story about this treasure?" asked Mike.

"Listen up, mon. Listen up. Me tell yu de story. Now listen real good . . ." and Andre proceeded to tell them about how his father had given him documents, and the map and money, and about Damian Henry and his rise through the ranks of the Shower Posse Cartel, and about giving the papers to a Professor, who wrote about the documents, and how it hit the newspapers in Jamaica, and Damian wanted the map so he could get the fortune to pay off the Arabs, who wanted to supply him with heroin from Afghanistan, and wanted to make the Shower Posse the biggest drug cartel in the world, and about his escape from Jamaica, leaving out only the death of Billy and his family.

"So these papers that your father found . . . you gave them to who?"

"De teacha, mon. Me arready tol yu dis."

"What's his name?"

"His last name be Dixon. Me remba from de papa, but me dunno de res."

"And where's the map?" asked Mike.

"Ah-ha," said Andre, and slapped his hand on the desk. "Yu no git de map til me git, wa yu say . . . amnesty."

"You're not getting amnesty," said Owens. "Not after all the murders you committed and all the drugs you've supplied. No way in hell!"

Andre sat back in the chair and folded his arms.

"Den yu don git de map."

Just then, Jake rose from his seat.

"You wait right here, Mr. Powell, if you would, please." He went to the door and went outside.

"Agent Parker . . . they find anything?"

"They've been working on it since they brought it in. I think this is what you're looking for," and she handed him an oilskin. Jake opened it and inside was a piece of leather. He smiled.

"Nice work, Agent Parker."

"Thank you, sir," she said, smiling back as she turned and walked down the hallway.

Jake re-entered the holding room.

"So, let me get this straight, Mr. Powell . . . you give us the map and we give you your freedom, you get amnesty for all your past crimes, and you go on your merry way?"

"See, dis bassmon, he git it. Dat be esactly right," said Andre.

"You wouldn't be talking about this map, would you?" Jake said, opening the oilskin and laying the piece of leather on the table.

The three men could see Andre shrink in front of them, his shoulders sag. The bravado left him, and he sat in silence, staring at the piece of leather.

"Arright, mon. Yu git me. Me git noting else. Wa happen to me now?"

"We're going to go talk outside, Andre," said Mike. "When we come back, we'll have an answer for you. Just sit tight."

Andre sat back in his chair.

"Like me git choice to do anyting else."

The three men then walked out of the room.

"Bring me up to speed, Mack," said Jake, "on this Shower Posse group. I've put a lot of them away, and I know they're bad. Do you have any idea what he's talking about?"

"I might. I can give you some facts and some rumors I've heard. There's no question the Shower Posse is the most powerful drug cartel in the Caribbean, but there's a group in Cuba that have made serious inroads into their trafficking, and the latest word is that the Posse has lost thirty percent of its revenue, which is a big hit for them to take. The problem in Jamaica is that there are two political parties. Norman Manley founded the People's National Party back in the late '30s and he used it in the '50s and '60s to gain independence for Jamaica, but an opposition party formed like it always does . . . The Jamaican Labor Party. They've been in and out of power since that time, and the trouble is extensive inroads have been made into that party by the Shower Posse, so what you really have in Jamaica is a government-sanctioned criminal enterprise.

"Just like Lansky wanted to have in Cuba," said Mike, looking at Jake.

"Pretty much," said Owens.

"But what about the Arabs? What is he talking about?" asked Jake.

"Here's where the rumor comes in. We know for a fact that ISIS has gained control of the Afghan poppy fields. They made a deal with the Taliban to give them protection and they've beaten the hell out of the Afghan regular forces who have tried to oppose them. The rumor is that ISIS is looking for one partner and one partner only in the Caribbean to whom they will guarantee direct delivery of all the heroin they can take, so long as the distribution system ensures ninety percent of the traffic goes into the United States."

"What would the outcome be?" asked Jake.

"It would be devastating," said Owens. "We'd have more heroin coming into this country than we could ever interdict and deaths would probably triple, which would be epidemic proportion."

"Looks like the terrorists are trying to find another way to strike at the homeland," said Mike.

"That's what everybody's thinking," said Owens, "but again, so far it's only rumor. We haven't been able to prove any of it."

"Well, why is this Damian so interested in this supposed treasure?" asked Mike.

"Because the other part of the rumor is that ISIS is requiring a half-billion dollar buy-in to get the exclusive contract – money that they're going to use to finance their terrorist operations, primarily against the United States, the destruction of which they see as their key to worldwide domination."

"So," said Jake, "if this treasure is not some pirate legend and really exists and Damian Henry gets his hands on it . . . ISIS will get exactly what it wants . . . a direct pipeline from Jamaica to the United States, with all the heroin they can supply."

"Exactly," said Owens, "and a fortune to carry out their attacks against us."

Mike looked at Jake.

"Please don't tell me we're walking into another 'save the world' scenario?"

"It is what it is," said Jake. "Let's go back and talk to our friend, Andre."

"All right, Andre, here's the deal," said Jake. "We're all going to get on a plane and head for Miami. Once we get you there, you're going to be turned over to Mr. Owens, here. He will guarantee your safety, but you're not going to be a free man. If what you've told us is true and because of you we end a bad situation, we may be able to work something out. You understand?"

Andre nodded his head.

"Me git yu, bassmon. Dat be it, den dat be it."

"All right. Let's get back to Miami.

"Mind if I catch a ride with you?" asked Mack.

"Be our guest," said Mike.

"Absolutely," said Jake, and they headed out to make arrangements.

"I'll catch up to you," said Owens. "I want to call one of my guys to meet us in Miami and set up transport. We'll get Mr. Powell here to a safe house, then probably move him to Quantico for safekeeping until all this is over.

"Sounds like a plan," said Jake. "See you at the plane."

CHAPTER 18

The flight back to Miami was uneventful, except for one phone call. Fifteen miles in, Jake's cell phone rang, and he answered.

"Jake, this is Jason Bates. Put me on speaker."

"Just a second, Jason."

"Mack, Mike, can you hear me?" said Jason.

"Loud and clear," said Mike, and under his breath, "unfortunately."

"Yeah, I'm here, Jason. What's up?" asked Mack.

"I'm in Miami. Once you get here, I need you three to come with me to Washington. The President has requested your presence at a meeting on this situation."

"What about Mr. Powell?" said Owens.

"I presume you're going to put him in protective custody?" asked Bates.

"That's the plan."

"Where are your men meeting you?"

"At Jake's office. We have a safe house nearby."

"All right. I'll meet you there and give you more information. Oh," said Bates, "and I assume you have the map Mr. Powell was talking about?"

"We have it, Jason," said Jake. "Don't worry."

"You know me, Jake," said Bates. "I always worry."

And with that, the line went dead.

"Well, it's official," said Mike. "We're in a worldwide crisis situation."

"No shit!" said Owens.

"Oh, you've gotten these calls before, too."

"Too many times to talk about," said Owens.

"I'm hurt," said Mike, "and here I thought it was only us."

"No, I'm sure Jason likes to spread the misery around."

"Who dat mon?" asked Andre.

"You don't want to know," said Mike. "Trust me."

"Yu peoples got deh crazy bassmon. Me tell yu."

"More than you know," said Jake, as the plane began its descent.

Tim Welsh, Mack Owens's right hand man was waiting for them when they arrived at the airport. After introductions were made, he ushered Jake, Mike, Mack, and Andre into the middle SUV in a three-vehicle caravan. The lead car having four DEA agents, and the backup car carrying Tim and three other agents.

Once everyone was in position, they started into Miami, following I95 from the airport down to the exit for NW Fifth Street and were just ready to turn to go onto Fourth when a large truck pulled out of an alley and blocked their progress.

Owens quickly looked in the rearview mirror and saw another vehicle had done the same behind them.

"Get out! It's an ambush!" he hollered, sending Jake, Mike, and Andre jumping to the ground.

The agents in the first car weren't so lucky, when an RPG launched from a twelfth-floor window across the street exploded into their vehicle, creating a fireball and leaving a mass of twisted wreckage, in which there would be no survivors.

Mack Owens was furious and rose to his feet just as men appeared from both vehicles that had blocked them front and back, firing automatic weapons at the survivors.

Mike, using the hood of the car for cover, returned fire with his Glock, and Owens yelled, "Anybody see where that RPG came from?"

"Yeah," said Mike, amid the gunfire. "Twelfth floor, left. See the curtains billowing where he knocked out the glass?"

Mack looked up and saw what Mike meant, and automatic fire or not, walked out into the street.

"Jesus Christ!" said Jake. "He's going to get killed!"

Mike yelled to the agents in the rear vehicle, "Cover him!" and they all began firing.

Mack stood there calmly, ignoring those firing, and waited. It was only a matter of seconds when the form reappeared in the window, the projectile clearly visible, as he reloaded. Then Mack fired repeatedly, hitting the projectile and causing it to explode into the room in which its operator had been concealed, destroying it and much of the floor on which the room was located.

Mack then turned his attention on the advancing men firing automatic weapons and downed two, as Mike hit a third, leaving only one, who fled back to his vehicle.

The agents in the rear had also been successful, driving back the approaching force, taking out two of the four, losing one of their own.

Unfortunately, it was a busy day in Miami and the sidewalks were crowded with civilians. It was later learned that Mary Ann Cutler died when a stray round struck her in the temple. Only quick-thinking by passersby saved her five-year old daughter, whom she was taking to the store to buy a party dress.

Rupert Jenkins, a bike delivery man, was the victim of being at the wrong place at the wrong time, speeding to a delivery at Jake's office when he turned the corner and entered a hail of gunfire that cut him down immediately.

There were three others that suffered minor wounds on a bright afternoon in the heart of Miami.

Mack Owens had gone back to the last vehicle to check on the downed agent. They could hear him screaming, "Who else knew about this? Who? Who did you talk to?"

"No one, Mack!" said Tim. "You know that!"

"Then how'd they know we'd be here? Five dead agents!" he yelled as he headed back to the middle vehicle. "Are all of you all right?" he asked.

"Yeah," said Mike. "I think we're okay," looking at Andre and Jake, who shook their heads affirmatively.

Still enraged, Mack banged his fist on the front of their vehicle.

"How the hell did this happen? Who did this?"

"It be Damian, bassmon," said Andre. "No doubt in me mind. Dis be his doin."

Just then, Jake's cell phone rang.

"What!" he snapped.

"Take it easy, mon," came the voice on the other end of the line. "Yu see wa dat Andre doz? Yu see all de death, de destruction he cause? Me tell yu wa, Mr. Sullivan, yu give him to me, along wid dat map he hab, a me let yu live. If naah, mo people die . . . me tell yu dat."

The anger grew in Jake as he replied, "Damian Henry, I presume?"

"Yu git it, mon," came the reply.

"Listen, you little son-of-a-bitch. You just declared war. You want a war? You're going to get one!"

"Shit, mon!" said Damian. "Yu people soft. Yu naah know wa war be . . . but me show yu. Me bring dat to yu . . . dat fa sure. Dat Andre . . . he still be alive?"

"I'm done talking to you, asshole," said Jake.

"Ah, he is . . . he is alive. Tell him naah fa long. Traitors to de Posse, dey hab short life spans, mon. His time be comin'. It be comin' soon."

"Fuck you!" said Jake, as he hung up the phone. Jake looked at the carnage around him. Police, firemen, and paramedics were all on the scene, and he saw the gurneys covered with sheets and the little girl crying in a policewoman's arms, and he looked at Mack and Mike and then at Andre. "Happy? Your friends did this," as he walked toward Andre.

"Easy, Jake," said Mike, getting in front of him.

Jake screamed and pointed directly at Andre, "You hear me! Your friends did this!"

"Nah, mon. Dese people naah my friends. Yu wanna know who be me friend? Billy . . . Billy be me friend since we little pinkneys. Dese people . . . yu waan know wa dey did to him? Dey slice him, beat him, to give dem dat map . . . den dey put his pinkneys in front of him a kill dem one by one to git him to talk . . . a den his wife . . . dey rape a dey kill her. And poor Billy, he canna talk. He canna talk 'cause he donna know whe de map be, 'cause me . . . me . . . me hid it at his ouse . . . a me naah tell him. So, me did it. Me kill my brudda, Billy. Dat my sin, but dis . . . nah . . . dis naah me. Nah more Posse. Me done. Nah more killin' . . . 'cept one . . . Damian. Him, me kill. Me promise yu dat."

Just then, Jason Bates walked up.

"Open warfare in the streets of Miami. God, this is a political nightmare for the President."

"Shut the hell up, Jason!" said Mike. "You see what happened here? We've got dead agents and civilians. You think we care about politics?"

"It's all politics, Mike, whether you like it or not. And you're part of it . . . so don't lecture me. Do what you need to do here, and then we have to catch a plane to Washington. The President of the United States is waiting." Then he walked away.

Mike just shook his head. "Son-of-a-bitch!" and all of them stood there in the street, not quite knowing what to do.

Just then, one of the surviving agents from the third car came running up to Mack.

"Sir, I found this on one of the dead attackers. From outward appearances, it appears they're all Jamaican, but we'll know more once we have a chance to analyze everything."

"Thanks, son," said Mack, as he looked at the phone. He noticed several calls to a certain number and punched it in. Then he heard a phone ring. He looked around and walked toward the sound, and then saw his friend and second in command looking at his pocket, a horrified expression on his face. Mack knew. "Answer it, Tim. Answer it, you son-of-a-bitch, before I shoot you down right now!"

Tim reached as if he was going to take the phone from his pocket, but instead pulled out a weapon from his waistband.

"Why answer it, Mack? Let's not play games. You know it was me."

"Why?" asked Mack. "How could you do this? Christ, these men were your friends . . . comrades."

"Cut the bullshit, Mack. You know why . . . the money. Don't you get it? We put our lives on the line every day fighting these bastards, and they're winning. Every inch we gain, they take back a foot . . . and for what? So we can die in the streets? So we can maybe make it and get a lousy pension to live on the rest of our lives? I'm tired of it, Mack. I'm tired of it. There was an opportunity, and I took it. And I'm not sorry I did."

"You're a Goddamn coward and a disgrace," said Mack, marching toward him.

"Stop where you are, Mack! One more dead agent doesn't mean a damn thing to me. I'm getting out of here."

But Mack kept moving.

"Have it your way, Mack," and just as he was ready to shoot, a shot rang out. Welsh looked stunned as he staggered and blood began to seep out from underneath his tie, spoiling his crisp, white shirt. He attempted to raise the weapon again and another shot rang out, and he fell to the ground.

Mack looked behind him and saw Jake standing there, the Glock he had taken from one of the dead agents in his hand, standing in a shooter's stance. Mack looked at him and nodded. Jake nodded back and threw the weapon to the ground and started walking, heading for his office a block away. Mack took Andre by the arm and followed, as did Mike, knowing that nothing more could be said.

CHAPTER 19

The carnage in Downtown Miami was still being cleared when Jake, Mike, Mack, and Andre Powell joined Jason Bates in a bullet-proof limousine and rode in an armed convoy back to the airport. They arrived safely and boarded a jet to Washington.

Landing in a restricted zone at Dulles International Airport, they were picked up by a similar convoy and taken to the White House. There was little talk on the way, given the events they had just been through. Even Jason Bates was in a somber mood and sat in silence throughout the flight.

They were turned over to the Secret Service at the entrance to the White House and, one by one, were ushered into the Oval Office.

Attorney General Lester Kirkland got up from his seat immediately and came over and shook Mike and Jake's hands.

"Glad to see you boys are all right. You, too, Mr. Owens. And this, I take it, is Mr. Powell?"

"That would be him," said Mike. "Good to see you again, Lester. Always seems to be under the same circumstances."

"I know, Mike. Unfortunately, it seems that way."

Marcus Turner, the head of the DEA, expressed sorrow at the loss of the five agents, but also told Mack how glad he was that he had survived, and that they were investigating how Tim Welsh had been contacted and turned, and how they would deal with the entire situation.

James Davis of the FBI was also present, as was the Director of the CIA, Janet Talmage. Extra chairs were brought in, and they all took seats. Just then, one of the paneled walls opened and in walked Jordon Fletcher, President of the United States, and all rose.

"Sit, everyone, sit," said President Fletcher as he took his seat behind the Resolute Desk.

Behind him came Jason Bates and a man that none of them recognized, and they took seats near the President's desk.

"Mr. Owens and Director Turner, I would like to express my and the country's sympathy on the death of five of your fine agents today. I have been briefed on the situation with Agent Welsh and directed Mr. Turner to conduct an investigation to see how security in the organization was breached and how he was turned by the cartel. If we find anyone else involved, I assure you, they will be dealt with swiftly and properly."

"Thank you, Mr. President," said both Turner and Owens, who had risen and now resumed their seats.

"Jake . . . Mike . . . I'm glad to see you got through this and that you made it safely here."

They also rose.

"Thank you, Mr. President," and then resumed their seats.

The President rose and then went around to the front of his desk and leaned back against it, his hands on the desk on either side of him, and crossed his legs.

"Gentlemen, it appears we have a crisis . . . a serious crisis, on our hands. Mr. Turner, Ms. Talmage . . . would you update everyone, please."

"Go ahead, Marcus. You go first," said Janet Talmage.

"We have hard evidence that ISIS is now in control of the Afghan poppy fields. They have agreed to provide security from all attacks and have agreed to give the Afghan's additional lands they have conquered to grow even more based upon obtaining exclusive production and distribution rights of the heroin that comes from those fields."

Janet Talmage then spoke.

"We have hard evidence that Damian Henry, the leader of the Shower Posse cartel in Jamaica, has joined the Cuban cartel and the Mexican cartels in bidding for an offer made by ISIS to all of them. That is, that ISIS will select one single cartel for distribution of heroin in the Caribbean Basin, so long as ninety percent of the heroin provided is guaranteed entry into the United States."

"And, Mr. President," said Turner, "that will triple the heroin inflow into this country with the attendant increase in use, criminal activity, and resultant deaths."

All were surprised as Andre Powell spoke out.

"Dat dere lady . . . she be full of shit!"

"How dare you!" exclaimed Talmage.

"Me tell yu, she be lying!"

"Mr. President . . ." said Talmage.

"Hold on a second, Janet. "You're making some serious allegations, Mr. Powell. You have information to back this up?"

"Hell ya! Me be dere when de CIA mon com. He meet wid Damian. He wanna buy him. He offer protection of de United States if Damian donna tek dis deal . . . protection fa de drugs to keep flowin'. Yur government, bassmon . . . dey gonna do dis if he donna go to de Arab bastards."

"Janet, is there any truth to this?" asked the President.

"Sir, as you know, we employ various mechanisms when we see a threat to try and diffuse that threat."

"Answer my question, Janet."

"It was one of the options we considered, Mr. President, but obviously, it didn't work."

"We'll talk about this later, Janet."

"Yes, Mr. President," she said, lowering her head.

"Jason, you want to let these people in on what we found out?"

"A Navy Seal team operating in Afghanistan captured a high-level ISIS official and through interrogation, we've learned that this situation is worse than we thought. What you have all said is correct, but there's more to it than that. ISIS's real goal in this matter, in addition to dramatically increasing the influx of heroin into this country, is to bring with it agents trained by them, be they Jamaican, Arabic, even disaffected United States citizens, to enter this country and recruit, using the heroin as an outreach program . . . so to speak . . . to gain the trust and dependency of young people in this country and turn them into terrorists. If this were to succeed, we would see random acts of terrorism on a weekly, if not daily, basis all across the United States. The calls for martial law, even military action, would begin and grow. There would have to be some type of response, and with those actions, gentlemen, there would be an erosion of rights. Civil liberties would be set aside to combat these threats, and it would be the end of democracy in this country as we know it. That is the true goal of ISIS in this matter. We have been successful through various means in dissuading the Cuban and Mexican cartels from proceeding. Our relationship with the Cuban government and the threat of armed intervention, if necessary, has led to a severe crackdown on the cartels in Cuba . . . a crackdown which will ease, to some degree, with a guarantee that there will be no acceptance of the proposal put forth by ISIS. The same has been done in Mexico, and we believe we have those organizations in check. Given the government in Jamaica being part of the problem, rather than the solution, we have no leverage. The only recourse we see is armed intervention by the United States military, which, of course, would destroy our relationship with the nations of Central and South America . . . and also spark who knows what actions by foreign powers.

We know at the present time that Damian Henry does not have the funds to accept the ISIS offer. Hence, his desperate attempt to obtain this treasure map, given the fact that he believes it to be true and legitimate and will lead him to the fortune he requires."

"Which," said President Fletcher, "leads us to the gentleman sitting here. This is Sir Anthony Bainbridge," said the President, "a Professor at Oxford University, who is an expert in seventeenth century documents. He has analyzed the documents Mr. Powell's father recovered at the Firefly Estate and gave to his son, who then turned them over to a Professor Dixon, I believe. Mr. Banebridge, would you please speak to your conclusions, having reviewed the various documents?"

"Thank you, Mr. President. I'd be happy to," said Sir Anthony Banebridge.

"This guy's like out of a movie," whispered Mike to Jake. And it was true. Banebridge was wearing a bow tie, a tweed jacket with leather patches on his elbows, and a pipe that could clearly be seen in his breast pocket . . . the caricature of an Oxford Don.

"I have reviewed the documents, and I have also looked at the alleged map, and I can say without equivocation the documents were not written by Sir Henry Morgan, and the map is someone's idea of a joke. It is simply gibberish."

Andre Powell jumped to his feet.

"Dat dere teacha be de fool," said Andre. "Dese papas, dey be real. Me fadda find dem at Firefly."

"That has no bearing on the matter, Mr. Powell, I assure you."

"Dat show jist how dum yu are," said Andre.

"Mr. Powell," said President Fletcher, "take your seat. Enough of the insults."

"Me tell yu wa, bassmon, yu go find de Professor . . . Professor Dixon. Bring him here. He prove to yu dat me be right. Me nah lie. Dere be a treasa, a yu best naah let Damian be de mon dat find it."

The President looked at Andre long and hard and silence enveloped the room.

"Mr. President," spoke Sir Banebridge, "I assure you I am correct in my analysis of these documents."

President Fletcher looked at Banebridge, walked over, and shook his hand.

"Professor, I greatly appreciate your efforts, and on behalf of the United States Government, I thank you. Jason, show the Professor out and make sure he gets safely to his hotel. Professor, I hope you have a safe trip home."

Banebridge cast an eye on Andre as he headed out the door, and if looks could kill, Andre would have died in his seat.

"Jason, come back in when you're done. Well, gentlemen, seems we need to hear from another party."

After several moments, Bates re-entered the room.

"Mr. President?" he asked.

"Find me Professor Dixon and get him here as fast as you can, please."

"I thought that's what you'd ask. I made a call while I was out and authorized a special deployment to bring Professor Dixon here from Jamaica. He should be here late this evening."

"Okay, gentlemen, I suggest we all have dinner here at the White House. We don't need any more comings and goings for the press to speculate upon in this matter, especially given the notoriety of some of our members," as he looked at Jake and Mike.

"We will then resume this evening when Professor Dixon arrives. Thank you."

And with that, the President started to leave the room.

"Excuse me, Mr. President," said Bates, "should I include Mr. Powell in our dinner plans?"

The President stopped and looked at Andre.

"He's the one who convinced me to call in Professor Dixon and send Professor Banebridge packing. I presume he's as hungry as the next man, so feed him."

And with that, the President was gone.

"Would you all please follow me? I'll find you a comfortable area where you all can wait while dinner is being prepared."

Jake, Mike, and Owens came up to Andre.

"You better be right about this, Andre," said Owens.

"Yu see. Andre nah lie. Dis be fa real, mon. De teacha, he com. He tell yu."

"I sure as hell hope so," said Jake.

Dinner was simple and buffet style – roast beef, potatoes, and green beans – simple fare, but since all were famished, delicious nonetheless. They tried to avoid the business at hand and made small talk while they ate – all except Andre, who acted like he hadn't seen food in a week, and for all they knew, maybe he hadn't. He was going back for more when Jason entered the room.

"Ladies and gentlemen, Professor Dixon has arrived. I suggest we reconvene."

Once again, they all rose to follow Jason Bates, except Andre, who was still at the buffet counter.

"Yu gotta eat, yu know."

"You've eaten enough for three people, and the President of the United States just asked you in. I think you better go," said Mike.

With a heavy sigh, Andre replied, "Arright, mon, arright. Me be comin'. . . me be comin.'" He put down his plate reluctantly and followed the others out of the room.

Once again, they were led into the Oval Office and resumed their prior seating arrangement and rose once again when the

President entered, this time with a small black man wearing frameless glasses and, also, a bow tie, with a well-worn jacket, absent the pipe.

Andre jumped up. "Bassmon, tank yu, tank yu fa comin'. Me tell dese people de udda teacha . . . he got it all wrong. He know nuttin'. Yu esplain to dem . . . dese tings be real."

"I'll do my best, Andre. And I'm sorry. I think I got you in a predicament by using your name in that article, referencing that a map exists."

"Yu don nuttin' wrong, Professor," said Andre. "Yu told de trut. Dat all yu can do," and he finished shaking the Professor's hand and sat back down.

"While you were eating, I had Professor Dixon look at the map supplied by Mr. Powell, and I think he's ready to discuss things with us. Professor Dixon, the floor is yours."

"Thank you, Mr. President. First, let me say I have great respect for my colleague, Professor Banebridge, but in this particular instance, I'm afraid he is wrong, simply because he does not understand how Captain Henry Morgan did things, how he prepared in advance, what a brilliant mind he was, and even more so, a brilliant tactician, how he prepared his papers, and what all this means. I must digress so that you understand.

There's not much early history regarding Henry Morgan. We know he was born in Whales. His name Morgan is from the old Welsh, meaning, fittingly, "of the sea" – and that is where Henry Morgan found his glory.

There are many stories about his origin. One has him coming to the New World as an indentured servant, working in Barbados as no more than a slave, until he joined the military and began the exploits for which he is famous. He sued a publisher who held that opinion for libel and won, so whether it's true or not, we do not know. Given his military prowess, however, it's more likely that he came to the New World in some form of military capacity, probably in Lord Cromwell's plan to invade Hispaniola, known as the 'Western Design', and quickly rose through the ranks – not so much in the forces of Great Britain, but in the world of privateers and pirates. We do know that he was involved in the invasion of Jamaica and the capture of Passage Fort and that he helped drive out the Spanish.

You have to understand that in Port Royal, Jamaica, in the 1600's, originated the first organized crime entity in the New World. The Brethern of the Coast were a group of privateers and/or pirates, because, unfortunately, even privateers operating under the sanction of the Crown went astray and performed acts of piracy, so the terms are rightfully confused. A man named Captain Edward Mansvelt was their leader and under him Morgan moved up in rank. When Mansvelt died, Morgan became the leader of The Brethern of the Coast and began a series of exploits that were unheard of prior to his arrival in the Caribbean ... and more importantly, made him the man most hated by the Spanish . . . and also, the most well-known and feared. You can read any history book on the Caribbean or on piracy and learn of his attacks on Portobelo, Cartagena, Maracaibo, and, of course, his most famous adventure . . . the attack on Panama City.

As I said, he was an astute tactician. He recognized the importance of Jamaica's location relative to the Windward Passage and the shipment of Spanish goods to the New and Old Worlds.

After his attack on Panama, he was taken to England in chains to be tried, and if convicted, hung for piracy. Two years later, he was knighted and back in Jamaica as Lieutenant Governor, Sir Henry Morgan, and served again as Acting Governor from 1680 until 1682.

He had married his cousin, Mary Elizabeth Morgan, the wealthy daughter of Edward Morgan, one of the island's former

Lieutenant Governors and his uncle, and cemented his position in Jamaican High Society.

When he died, he owned many estates on the island and was extremely wealthy for his time.

I tell you all this so you understand the type of man that you're dealing with.

Now, to the matter at hand.

To authenticate the documents given to me by Andre, you have to compare them to other documents. The same is true of the map. A man by the name of Bartholomew, and that's all we know from history as to his name, was Henry Morgan's right-hand man. He created many of the charts that Morgan used in sailing the Caribbean. If you compare the lettering on those charts, you'll see that letters are clearly the same as letters on the documents provided to me by Andre."

He spread the charts out on the table between the two couches in the Oval Office and invited all to look.

"Look at the 'M' on Morgan's Map and look at the 'M' on Maracaibo . . . clearly done by the same hand."

"Wait a minute," said Jake. "I'm sorry, Professor Dixon, but if I hear you correctly, all that proves is that Bartholomew wrote the documents, not that Morgan did."

"Correct, Mr. Sullivan. Correct. And he did. Bartholomew wrote the first drafts of the documents, dictated to him by Henry Morgan. Morgan wrote a letter to his wife, and in that letter, he explained that he didn't have time to keep up with all of his correspondence, and his good and truthful man, Bartholomew, wrote everything for him, except for the final product, which Morgan did in his own hand. Here's a copy of that letter. Here's a copy of the first draft of documents that Morgan hadn't gotten to yet, and here are documents that have been edited into the final drafts. Compare the lettering on the first draft documents with Bartholomew's on the map and on the charts and the documents that are in final draft to Morgan's writing in the letter to his wife. Again, I believe you will find they are identical.

I have every belief and faith that these documents are the documents of Henry Morgan, as is that map, prepared by his true and faithful servant, Bartholomew, and/or Henry Morgan, himself."

"Professor," asked Mike, "what's the significance of this Firefly place?"

"Firefly is an estate on a promontory overlooking Port Maria. It was the home of the playwright, Noel Coward, who purchased it and built a home there and renovated the grounds. On those grounds was a stone building, open air, with walls in some places ten feet thick. It was a lookout point for Henry Morgan. From it he could oversee the Windward Passage. There is also a hole in the ground that still exists close to the gravesite of Noel Coward, somewhat overgrown probably at the present time, but, it was the beginning of a tunnel that went down to a cave that opened onto the beach at Port Maria. Morgan held it out to be an escape route to his men, but I believe it was more than that, and this map confirms it."

"How so, Professor?" asked the President.

Turning to President Fletcher, Dixon went on, "Because, Mr. President, I believe that passage is the beginning of a route used by Henry Morgan to move the entire plunder of the City of Panama secretly to somewhere in Port Royal, probably a warehouse, to be stored there until he was ready to launch one of the most elaborate plans ever conceived in the New World.

In short, Mr. President, I believe that near Port Royal on the Island of Jamaica, there is a fortune, worth probably in excess of one-half billion dollars, and I believe that is what Damian Henry is after."

CHAPTER 20

"Let me elaborate just a bit more," said Dixon. "I've made copies of the map for all of you. Now understand that in January of 1671, Henry Morgan, sailing his flagship 'Satisfaction', sailed across the Caribbean to the Isthmus of Panama, marched through the jungle to cross the Isthmus and attack the City of Panama on the Pacific side. The legend has always held that he missed his opportunity in seizing one of the greatest fortunes ever accumulated by allowing a great deal of it to sail out to sea before he could actually attack the city. It is my belief that rumor was started by Morgan, himself. His ship, the Satisfaction, and four others, sailed onto a reef outside the Chagres River, after the Fortress of San Lorenzo had already been captured. Henry Morgan was one of the finest seaman of his day, and to allow five ships in his fleet, including his own, to flounder on a reef, makes no sense.

We also know that it's true he left in the dead of night in another ship he had commandeered and left most of the crew to guard the Fortress at San Lorenzo, knowing full well that the Spanish would obtain reinforcements and massacre those men. But if you presume that Morgan had a long-term plan that required ultimate secrecy, losing most of his crew would be just what he wanted. I believe he had other ships waiting and that much of the wealth taken from the City of Panama was marched by a group of different men under his command through a different path to those ships somewhere else on the coast, which ships were then sailed back to Port Maria."

"But where did it go, Professor?" asked Mike. "How does that much wealth suddenly just disappear?"

"Again, I told you, Morgan was a master strategist. I think he envisioned the grand scheme of this endeavor before he ever left for Panama, and I think he made preparations before he ever left for Panama. If you look at the map, you see that there is no inland waterway by which he could have sailed from Port Maria to Port Royal. He couldn't arrive in triumph in Port Royal because everyone would know then just how much he had obtained, and, of course, it would have been claimed by the Crown.

So, how does he get all this wealth from Port Maria to Port Royal? He can't march it through the hills and valleys of the jungle. It would have taken forever and most of his men would have died. But let us assume that the path from his lookout to the cave on the beach at Port Maria somehow led to a system of caves that crossed Jamaica at the base of the Blue Mountains. Suppose he was able to somehow, through a connection of caves, make his way from the north shore to the south shore of the island. He could have done it all in secret, over as much time as it took, and that wealth may very well still be sitting in a warehouse in what was Port Royal."

"What do you mean 'what was Port Royal', Professor?" asked Jake.

"There was a disastrous earthquake that struck Port Royal in June of 1692 that destroyed two-thirds of the city and killed half the population. The sand on which the buildings along the water sat became liquefied when the earth opened up and the water overcame it, and the buildings simply slid into the Caribbean. A resultant tsunami occurred, taking the water a mile out from shore and bringing it back in a wave in excess of six feet high, covering everything that had gone into the sea with at least ten feet of water. If this warehouse to which this wealth was delivered is where I think it may have been, it would presently be under water."

"Then how do we get to it?" asked Mike.

"That, I can not tell you," said the Professor. "I am only sure that it is still there."

"Professor," said Jake, "you indicated that the map confirmed your suspicion. I'm looking at this. How so?"

"Look at the first line of the clue. 'Look out and follow the path.' Morgan's stone fortification on the cliffs above Port Maria was known as 'The Lookout'. 'Follow the path' from the lookout would mean 'the escape tunnel' down to the cave at Port Maria. It makes sense. It would be an easy place to offload the ships in the dead of night, unseen by others, especially if guards were set so that no one could get close.

The second line, 'that leads to satisfaction' – the name of Morgan's flagship – 'once lost, now found' – a reference, I believe, to the riches of Panama. 'Lift me up and push on', I can't tell you what that means. That's the one clue I haven't been able to decipher. It may be the key to the entire thing, but 'the riches of Sodom' is easy. Port Royal, at the time of the earthquake of 1692, was second only to Boston as the largest city in the New World. There were supposedly sixty-five hundred people there before the earthquake. Most of them – businessmen, prostitutes, pirates, goldsmiths, tavern keepers, and other artisans and merchants – there were over two thousand buildings crammed into over fifty acres of real estate, and there were two hundred ships visiting the port every year. It was the home port of all the pirates of the Caribbean, and because of the open debauchery on its streets, it came to be known as the 'Sodom' of the New World. 'The riches of Sodom shall be yours' says the map – that's where the wealth of Panama was taken, and that's where it remains to this day. Of that, I have no doubt.

I apologize, ladies and gentlemen, if I have been long-winded, but I think you needed to understand why I believe my conclusion to be true. It's based not just on these papers, although they clearly establish what I believe to be the truth, but based upon my knowledge of the man."

"One question, Professor," said Mack Owens. "What was Morgan's grand plan?"

"It's amazing in its scope, actually," said the Professor, warming up to giving a lecture on Jamaican history. "He was going to use the money he had taken from Panama and, in effect, return it . . . give it back to the Spanish as a buy-in, for which the Spanish would name him Governor of all Spanish Lands in the Caribbean – Cuba, Hispaniola, The Spanish Main, and Panama – all would be under his jurisdiction. He would then take over Jamaica by force, if necessary, and believed he could convince the British that they should afford him the same title, and he would then become Governor General of the Caribbean and all the dominions therein, bringing, as he says in his writings, peace and prosperity to the region for the benefit of all, with no more acts of piracy or war between the parties.

His last entry was in May of 1688. Three months later in August, he was dead. His plans never materialized, and his fortune never moved."

"His men, wouldn't they know where it was?" asked Mike.

"Not if I know Morgan. In addition to being a master tactician, he was also ruthless. I believe those men lie, to this day, somewhere in the caves, dead, as well as his faithful Bartholomew. There is truth to the adage, gentlemen, and lady, that 'dead men tell no tales.'"

CHAPTER 21

With that, Professor Dixon sat down, and everyone looked at each other, taking in all that he had said. Finally, President Fletcher spoke.

"Professor, I thank you, and I must tell you, you have me convinced. More importantly, I believe Damian Henry is convinced, and if there is any chance whatsoever that this treasure exists, and any chance whatsoever that it could fall into his hands, he must be stopped, and I believe we can best do that by finding the treasure ourselves."

"Here we go," whispered Mike to Jake.

"Mr. Sullivan, Mr. Lang . . . this office is going to call upon you once again. I want you to take Mr. Owens and Professor Dixon and go to Jamaica. Unlock the secrets of this map and find the treasure. You will have whatever resources you need."

"Understood, Mr. President," said Jake, rising.

"Mr. President, if I may," said Professor Dixon, rising to his feet, "there is a system of technology that would be very helpful in this task, but it is very expensive."

"Professor Dixon, I said you would have whatever resources you need. Make any arrangements required with Mr. Bates, my Chief of Staff. God's speed, gentlemen."

CHIP BELL

"Wait jist de minute!" said Andre. "Dis information all com from me Fadda a me. Dis bastard, dis Damian Henry, he be de one dat kill me best friend . . . me brudda, Billy, a butcher his family. Me need to go. Me know de land. Me know de peoples. Me be a help, a me promise, when de job be done, me belong to Mr. Owens a de DEA, to do whateva he need to do. So, please, me beg, lef me go. Me need to do dis . . . fa Billy."

President Fletcher looked at Jake and Mike and Mack.

"Gentlemen, your call."

They looked at each other, and it was Mike who spoke.

"Let him come, sir. If I was him, I'd be begging you to go, too."

The President looked at Jake and Owens and they shook their heads in agreement.

"Very well, Mr. Powell. I'm releasing you in the custody of these gentlemen. You will listen to them and obey them. Should you attempt to escape them in any way, they have my full authorization to shoot you on the spot. Do you understand?"

"Me do. Tank yu, tank yu, sir. Tank yu, bassmon, vedy, vedy much."

"Do me proud, Mr. Powell, that'll be thanks enough. All of you, do me proud . . . do this country proud."

And with that, the President left the room.

"Figure out what you need, gentlemen," said Bates, "and let me know, and we'll get it for you. I don't have to tell you, time is of the essence. You're in a race with a very bad man . . . a race you need to win," and then he exited.

"He's always great at a pep talk, isn't he?" said Mike.

Mack laughed and nodded his agreement.

"Professor, gentlemen, let's sit down and figure out what we need and how we're going to do this."

"So, Professor, you really think he went through caves, huh?" asked Mike.

"I'm almost positive of it, Mr. Lang."

"Damn shame."

"What do you mean?" asked Jake.

"We're going to one of the most beautiful islands in the Caribbean – palm trees, sand, those little drinks with umbrellas – and we're going to spend all our time underground in dark, wet caves. I should have known," he said, looking at Jake, "just a normal vacation with you."

"Quit your complaining. If we find the treasure, I promise I'll buy you a drink with a little umbrella, all right?"

"Okay," said Mike. "That works."

And they began to go over their plans.

THE PIRATE TREASURE HUNT

CHAPTER 22

It took several weeks before they were ready to head to Jamaica. President Fletcher was true to his word and plans were put into place to install the Swiss-designed system that the Professor requested, which would allow him to use a locator beneath Jamaica's surface.

A fake corporation was established through the United States intelligence agencies, which bought the equipment from the Swiss and then made contact with the necessary parties in the Jamaican government, indicating that due to the tectonic and seismic conditions in Jamaica, it was the perfect spot for them to test out their new technology, and they were willing to pay a substantial fee for a temporary right to install towers above the cave system at the base of the Blue Mountains, and they would cause no ecological harm and remove the towers and all other equipment as soon as the project was completed.

Their assurances really weren't necessary once they indicated they were willing to pay for their testing.

Once the contracts were signed, a military unit posing as contractors from the phony corporation entered Jamaica and set up the towers pursuant to the Professor's specifications at the locations he designated.

During these weeks, Jake and Mike were back in Miami delegating cases, closing investigations, and otherwise clearing their calendars.

Andre was kept safe at the DEA section at Quantico, much to his displeasure, and Mack was making sure his Jamaican contacts were still in play.

When it was finally time for the group to depart, the other issue was widespread concerns about the penetration of the Jamaican Government by the Shower Posse cartel. It was determined by the security analysts in Washington to keep the contacts in Jamaica to a minimum. Mack Owens had insisted that they deal directly with the contact he had made in the Jamaican Constabulary Force's Narcotics Division, and after explaining the contact's position and his knowledge of this individual, the powers that be agreed.

Accordingly, their arrival at Norman Manley International Airport, by private jet rather than Air Jamaica, was late at night and was met by Owens' contact, the Senior Superintendent of the Narcotics Division, Antwon Williams.

After all their gear was unloaded into a nondescript van, they boarded the vehicle and were taken by Williams to an old, abandoned hanger, which had been set up as a command post by Williams and those on his staff that he trusted.

"Not quite as plush as your offices at 101 Old Hope Road," laughed Owens.

"Not even close, Mack," said Williams, "but nothing is kept secret in Kingston, so we're far better off here."

Just then, one of Williams' officers came up to greet them.

"Mr. Sullivan . . . Mr. Lang . . ."

"Thanks, Superintendent, but I know the other three," said the officer. "How are you, Mack?"

"Doing fine, Sargent, and you?"

"Hanging in there," said Bennett. He extended his hand to Professor Dixon. "Professor, good to see you again."

"My pleasure, officer," said Dixon.

"Mr. Sullivan, Mr. Lang, I'm Sargent Emmanuel Bennett," and then looked directly at Andre Powell. "And this one," said Bennett, "I've been hunting him for a long time."

"Yah, mon," said Powell, "but now, yu see me be on de side of de angels."

"Like hell you are," said Bennett.

"All right, Sargent . . . that'll do," said Williams. "We're here to fully cooperate with these gentlemen and help them on their mission. Understood?"

"Sir," said Bennett, "I'm telling all of you . . . keep an eye on this one. Don't believe a single thing he says."

"Nah, mon," said Andre. "Dat be any way to treat a good guy?", laughing.

"Be careful, boy, or I'll shove that laugh down your throat," said Bennett, turning and walking away.

"Sorry about that," said Williams. "He's lost a lot of good men dealing with the Shower Posse. No one anyone around here has much regard for you, Mr. Powell."

Andre just shrugged and looked away.

"Mack, gentlemen, it's late. We've cordoned off a section of this hanger. There are cots and a shower and toilet facility. There's a stocked refrigerator, hot plate, and I think everything else you'll need to spend the night."

"Sounds like it's four star," said Mike.

Williams laughed. "No, not quite, Mr. Lang, but I'll feel a lot better with you here. I have this area completely sealed off and under guard by men I trust . . . and hopefully, no one knows you're here. My men will get all your gear unloaded and get you set up, and then you can get some sleep. Sargent Bennett and his crew will get you safely to Port Maria, and you can start your hunt."

"Sounds good, Antwon," said Mack, and they shook hands.

Jake extended his.

"Thank you, Superintendent. We appreciate all the help."

"My pleasure," said Williams. "If Damian Henry gets his hands on that money, he'll own this island, and God knows what'll happen then." And with that, he called his men over to help stow the new arrivals' gear.

As the van had passed through the airport to their destination, no one had paid much attention to the man on the movable scaffold, working on the single engine plane in one of the hangers along their route, nor had they noticed when he left the scaffold and took up a position along the entrance to his hanger with a telescopic lens aimed at the passengers as they exited the van.

CHAPTER 23

They rose early, showered, and dressed and were waiting for Bennett when he arrived. He directed two of his men to get their backpacks and duffle bags and load them into the van with the rest of their gear as they headed outside.

It was a warm and sunny, beautiful morning in Jamaica.

"Ah," said Mike, stretching, "another vacation in the beautiful Caribbean, only interrupted by the occasional murder and mayhem."

"Something we'd like to avoid," said Jake.

"Yeah, right," said Mike under his breath, as he took a walk to exercise his cramped muscles.

After all the gear had been stowed and everyone was ready, they loaded into the van, with one of Bennett's men driving and him sitting in the front passenger's seat. They proceeded from the airport and drove along the Palisadoes, the narrow strip of ground that formed the natural breakwater for Kingston Harbour.

"You know," said Professor Dixon, "if we were going the opposite direction and reached the end of this bit of land, we'd be at our destination, Port Royal."

Jake took another sip of Blue Mountain coffee from the styrofoam cups that had been provided by Sargent Bennett.

"Here's to safe passage and to finding what we're looking for."

"Amen to that," said Owens.

Aside from some small talk between Bennett and the group, they drove in silence as they reached the A4 and skirted Kingston and then headed through its center on the A3.

Their scenery on the ride north was breathtaking, with the Blue Mountains rising to their right and dense tropical foliage surrounding them. They crossed small streams and saw waterfalls that plunged from steep, craggy hillsides. Jamaica's nickname as 'the land of wood and water' was truly fitting.

They stopped in Castleton, home of the Botanical Gardens, for more coffee and johnny cakes, one of Jamaica's breakfast delicacies, and then proceeded on until they reached the coast at Annotto Bay. They continued northwest on the A3 along the coast to Port Maria.

During their drive, Professor Dixon had been intently working on his laptop, raising his head only so often and then staring out the window, smiling and then going back to work. It was only when they arrived in Port Maria and he had directed Sargent Bennett to his offices that he shut his laptop and looked at the group.

"President Fletcher is a man of his word," he said. "All the necessary towers along the route I planned have been erected, as he had promised."

"Did you test everything, Professor?" asked Jake.

"I did, and the signals are loud and clear."

"Did Bates send you the codes we had talked about?"

"He did," said the Professor, and I've entered them and verified them. One tap and they'll go out."

"Good," said Jake, nodding his head.

After their gear was unloaded and moved into Professor Dixon's office, Sargent Bennett was ready to leave. Shaking each of their hands, except, of course, for Andre, Bennett bid them goodbye.

"I'll have men in the area. You've entered my number in your phones. If anything at all comes up, call me and we'll come to your aid. I'd still rather come with you and have some of my men closer."

"Can't do it," said Jake. "The way the Posse operates with its web of informants, my guess is they know we're here already . . . but they'll sure as hell know with you tagging along with us, given your status in the narcotics division."

Mack Owens extended his hand.

"You've done enough, Sargent. Thanks for getting us here in one piece, but we have to take it from here."

Bennett reluctantly nodded.

"Understood. Good luck. Call if you need me."

"Thanks."

And with that, Bennett re-entered the van and his driver pulled away.

CHAPTER 24

"Gentlemen, wait one second while I make a call and I'll see if our rooms are ready at the Casa Maria," said the Professor, as they crowded into his small office filled with papers, books, and maps. The walls were covered with certificates from the Jamaican Historical Society, The National Heritage Trust, and the Jamaican Caves Organization.

"James . . . yes, I'm back. We made it safely and I'm in the office. Are the rooms ready? Fine, thank you, James. We'll be there shortly." Professor Dixon clicked off his phone and looked at the others. "My assistant, James, has everything ready at the hotel whenever you're ready to leave."

"Teacha, wa be dese crazy maps?" asked Andre.

"Geological surveys of the cave systems on the island."

Mike had been walking around, looking at the titles on the books bulging from the shelves.

"Looks like you dabble in a little bit of everything, Professor . . . history, geology, botany."

Professor Dixon sighed.

"Yes, Jamaica has so many things to offer. My dream has always been to create one cultural center on the island where everyone could come and learn about the amazing things that this island holds, but, unfortunately, money is so desperately needed for other things that government funding is an impossibility, and we don't have generous donors as you have in the United States. So, for now, I do what I can with what I have . . . and every once in a while I get someone like James. He's been coming here since he was a young boy. He couldn't even read, but I could tell that he wanted to learn . . . and he did. I think he's come to know as much about all these subjects as I have. Hopefully, someday, he'll take over for me and maybe he'll make my dream a reality."

"So what exactly is this cave system we are about to enter?" asked Jake. "And what was it the President had set up to help us?"

Professor Dixon's eyes lit up, as he clearly enjoyed teaching the wonders of his island to others.

"You have to understand that two-thirds of Jamaica is covered by caves riddled through yellow and white limestone. The big river caves are in the center of the island where there's been, more or less, complete erosion of the stone. Then in what is called the 'cockpit area' there are sink holes that go deep into the limestone bed but don't cover a great area. The cave system that we are going to be following is in the area of the Portland Ridge, and these are large, horizontal caves, similar to what you have in Kentucky and New Mexico's Carlsbad Caverns. As I said, I think Morgan found a way through those caves, and that's how he moved his treasure from the north to the south side of the island."

"See, bassmon . . . me tell yu dat teacha be right mon fa de job. He know de island inside a out."

"It appears he does," said Jake.

"And what about this system that you wanted, Professor?" asked Owens.

"Ah, yes. I explained to Mr. Bates that an underground system had been developed by the Swiss where transmitters placed above ground over the caves connect to GPS satellites in the normal way. Those transmitters receive signals from a special transmitter that

I'll be carrying, and I can then triangulate signals to provide an accurate position. That's what I was working on during the drive up here . . . the transmitter provided to me by Mr. Bates . . . making sure that the above ground transmitters had been installed and, at least, above ground, the system was working properly."

"What're the odds it will work once we're down in some dark hole?" asked Mike.

The Professor smiled.

"Only time will tell, Mr. Lang, only time will tell."

"Great," murmured Mike under his breath, "just great."

"Well, gentlemen, my van is parked just across the street," said the Professor. "Shall we load up our belongings and head for the hotel and a night of rest and a good meal before we begin our adventure tomorrow morning?"

Jake looked at Mike, Mack, Andre, and then Professor Dixon.

"Lead the way, Professor."

They then gathered up their gear and headed out.

As the van pulled away, heading for the Casa Maria, a man sitting on a bench in front of a tavern four doors down from the Professor's office took out his cell phone, punched in a number, and began to talk.

CHAPTER 25

They arrived at the Casa Maria Hotel after only a ten minute drive on the Coastal Highway. The quaint pink and lime green-painted structure was separated from the Caribbean by a neatly trimmed green lawn that seemed to run directly into Little Bay. It was comprised of only twenty rooms and was so situated that it faced directly east into the cool trade winds. Isolated, with no nearby commercial activity, the surf crashing on the nearby reef was the only sound.

As the Professor's van drove up, a young man came racing down the steps and embraced the Professor as he exited the driver's seat.

"James, my boy! Good to see you! How are you?"

"Hi, Professor. Fine. How was your trip?"

"Exhilarating but somewhat tiring, James. Let me introduce you," and introductions were made between James Smalley, the Professor's assistant, and Jake, Mike, Mack, and even Andre.

"I've heard a lot about you," said Jake.

"And I, you, Mr. Sullivan," as he shook Jake's hand, and then Mack's and Mike's. Andre leaned against the van, his arms crossed.

"So, yu be de teacha's boy, huh?" he asked.

James stiffened.

"I'm the Professor's assistant."

"Yu still be workin' fa de bassmon, boy," said Andre, brushing past him and walking up the steps to the hotel.

James looked after him as he went and then looked back at the Professor.

"If it hadn't been for you, Professor, that could have been me."

"Well, it's not you, James," said the Professor.

"I know," said James, "but I just want you to know how much I appreciate everything you've done for me and how much you mean to me."

"My, my, James . . . absence does make the heart grow fonder. That's fine . . . that's fine. Now, what say we get these bags unloaded and to our rooms, shall we?"

"Certainly, Professor," said James, and started to unload the van.

CHAPTER 26

The Professor had booked one of the balconies overlooking the sea for dinner. It was an amazing setting – the cool trade winds blowing in and the brilliant orange-pink colored sky being painted by a setting sun in the west, palm trees slightly bending in the breeze, and the smell of flowers planted throughout the twenty-five acres the hotel commanded.

They arrived one by one and took their seats, the last being Mike, who walked in from the bar carrying a Red Stripe beer, the moisture coming off it as its coldness contacted the warmer air.

"Nice bar," he said, as he took his seat, looking at Jake. "Called the 007, with the James Bond logo, the seven looking like a gun."

"Aptly named," said the Professor. "Ian Fleming wrote James Bond novels at his estate just down the beach, and Sean Connery spent many a night drinking and dining here."

"Really?" said Mike.

"Yes," said the Professor. "Tomorrow we'll go to Firefly, Noel Coward's estate up on the bluff, that was visited by Katharine Hepburn, Errol Flynn, Richard Burton, and Queen Elizabeth, herself."

"A lot of action in this little part of the world," said Mike.

"I told you," said the Professor, "Jamaica has many secrets that need to be told to the world."

"Watch what you ask for," said Mack. "I'm sorry, but the isolation gives this place its beauty. You don't want to make it into another tourist trap."

"Ah, correct, Mr. Owens," said the Professor. "That is the constant battle of the Historical and Cultural Trust of this island with the government. All they care about is tourist dollars, rather than the rich history and culture of the island."

"I'm afraid it's the way of the world," said Jake. "Ask anyone in Key West and they'll tell you the same thing."

"Dat easy to say, Professor. Yu don live in de shitholes of dis island whe de poor people live. Yu talk 'bout de Shower Posse wid de hatred, but if de government do wa it suppose to do, dere be nah need fa de Shower Posse. We only git de people wa dey waan 'cause dey got no hope."

The Professor looked long at Andre.

"You have a valid point, Mr. Powell . . . very insightful and very valid . . . but enough government and politics. Let's enjoy this beautiful evening. Shall we order?"

The seafood that they had ordered was delicious and they were halfway through their meal when Jake's cell phone rang.

"Probably Bates," said Mike, "wanting to know if we found the treasure yet," and they all laughed.

"Hello," said Jake.

"Put de phone on speaka, bassmon," came the response.

Jake's face changed as he looked at the rest of the group, and everyone put down their utensils and stared.

"All right," Jake said as he put the phone on speaker and set it on the table, "who is this?"

"Com on, Mr. Sullivan. Yu be de great detective. Surely yu can figure dis out."

"It be Damian," said Andre.

"Ah, little Andre be wid yu. Yu be back on de island, huh, boy? Good. We hab bidness, yu a me."

"Yah, we got bidness," said Andre. "Yu mek de big mistake, Damian . . . butcha me brudda. Yu gonna pay fa dat."

There was a loud laugh from the speaker.

"Tell dat fool boy to be quiet. Now, yu listen to me, Mr. Sullivan. Dis be yur last chance. Me waan de Professor a me waan de map . . . a den yu all go home . . . 'cept fa Andre . . . he stay so we do our bidness. Wa yu say?"

"I'll tell you what he says," said Mike, "go fuck yourself!"

"You heard him," said Jake.

"Americans . . . yu tink yu know evyting, Yu tink yu run evyting. Yu tink yu buy evyting. Dis me island. Me be de bassmon here . . . a me can git to yu wheneva me want to. Just rememba . . . yu had de chance. Now yu see."

And with that, there was a loud explosion and a ball of flames from the parking lot as the Professor's van exploded, debris flying everywhere, black smoke rising into the air obscuring the twilight of a beautiful night.

"Yu see? Any time. But yu neba know when me comin' fa yu," and with that, the line went dead.

The Professor's head was in his hands.

"My van."

"Professor, I'm so sorry," said James.

"It's all right, James. Don't worry about it. We'll find a way to replace it."

"I'm really starting to hate this son-of-a-bitch," said Mike.

"You and me both," said Mack.

"I'm heading for the bar. Buy you a beer?"

"Absolutely," said Mack.

"Listen, before you go, from now on . . . we don't talk about anything around anyone. Who knows who's working for Damian. When we talk, we do it out in the open . . . no one around."

"Got it," said Mike, and he and Mack walked under the 007 sign to the bar.

"Well, Andre, what do you make of it?" asked Jake.

"Damian love terrorizin' people. He lovin' dat dey be fraid of him. He right. He kill us anytime him waan, but right now, him just waan us know he here."

"I suspected as much," said Jake. "Let him play his game. We still have the trump card."

"Wa be dat?" asked Andre.

"That one," said Jake, getting up from his chair, "I'm keeping to myself."

CHAPTER 27

The next morning, after they had arisen and had a small breakfast, they went outside to find Sargent Bennett leaning against a Land Rover, waiting for them.

"What's this?" asked Mike.

"It's our new ride," said Jake. "I called the good Sargent last night and made arrangements."

"Nice work," said Owens, as Sargent Bennett threw the keys to Jake.

"It's not armored, but at least it has bullet-proof glass. It's the best I could do on such short notice."

"That'll work," said Jake. "Thanks, Sargent. I appreciate it."

"Look, Jake, are you sure you don't want me and my men to go with you?"

"No," said Jake. "Look, if Henry wants to get to us, he'll get to us. All we can do is focus on the job we're here to do and not put anyone else in danger."

"Yeah, but that's our job."

"I know that, Sargent, and I appreciate it, but this is the way it is going to be."

"All right, Mr. Sullivan. It's your call."

"I appreciate everything you've done for us. Let's leave it at that for now, all right?"

"Be careful," Sargent Bennett said, walking away. "Watch your back."

"Don't worry," said Mike, "that's my job."

"And mine," said Owens, smiling at Mike.

"Let's get our gear stowed and be on our way."

CHAPTER 28

After their gear was loaded, Jake, Mike, Professor Dixon, James, Mack Owens, and Andre headed out to the Firefly Estate above the bluffs of Port Maria. Professor Dixon directed Jake as they headed up the Coastal Highway to a turnoff on a secondary road and then on to a narrow road filled with potholes and debris, that wound its way up to the top of Look Out Hill. The actual turn-off into Firefly was like a tropical rainforest with low-hanging trees, plants, and flowers into a vast expanse of cultivated lawn. A small white cottage, and another stone structure sat on the very summit of the hill.

After the vehicle was parked and they exited, Mack Owens asked, "So this is Firefly?"

"Yes," said Professor Dixon. He looked at James. "James, you want to tell them the history of this place?"

"I'd love to, Professor," said James. "For many years now, this estate has been in the hands of the Blackwell Family. You may have heard of Chris Blackwell . . . a son of the original owners, who founded Island Records and introduced the world to the music of Jamaica through Bob Marley. In addition to this property, the Blackwells own various lands along the beach.

One parcel ten miles away was sold to the British author, Ian Fleming, which he named 'Golden Eye'. It was Fleming who introduced Noel Coward to Jamaica, and he bought a seven-acre seaside site and built 'Blue Harbour', his home for several years. However, because of all the comings and goings of all his friends, he could not write or create, so in 1956 he bought the Firefly property from Mrs. Blackwell and built the small, white stucco, English style house you see here. The large stone structure over there was servants' quarters and a bar. It now is a concession stand for visitors. That stone structure was originally the lookout for Captain Henry Morgan. The men walked through the estate to the edge of the cliff and looked out at the panorama that included the far reaches of the Caribbean Sea, with the Blue Mountains rising through the clouds in the east."

"I can see why he'd want to come here," said Jake. "Who owns it now?"

"After Sir Noel's death in 1973, the house was in great disrepair. Chris Blackwell came in and did renovations, and the entire estate is now operated by the Jamaican National Heritage Trust."

Jake looked at the Professor.

"One of your organizations, correct?"

"Indeed, it is," said the Professor. "I told you . . . many secrets has this island."

"There's no question it's beautiful," said Mike, "but we have a secret of our own to figure out. Where do we go from here, Professor?"

"Let's go over here to Sir Noel's grave site."

They followed the Professor past the plaque in the ground commemorating Sir Noel Coward's burial place toward shrubbery off on the side. Right at the edge was a grate bolted into the ground, covering what appeared to be a hole in the otherwise manicured lawn.

"This," said the Professor, "is allegedly the beginning of the secret tunnel Captain Henry Morgan created so he could escape to the coast, if need be, and sail out into the Windward Passage."

Mack Owens went over and tested the padlock.

"Looks like we're locked out."

"Good thing then, Mr. Owens, that I have the key," said the Professor, bending down and inserting it, and with some difficulty, opening the lock and lifting the grate cover to the side, as the rusty hinges squealed in the otherwise quiet setting.

Jake noticed Andre standing with his back to them, looking at the estate and out over the Caribbean.

"What's the matter, Andre?" he asked.

Without turning, Andre spoke.

"Be de same all de time on dis island. De rich, white folks come . . . de beautiful ouses . . . fancy hotels . . . but no matter how much de money com to de island, it neva reach de people."

Then he turned on Jake.

"Just like dis treasa. All dat money . . . if we find it, who yu tink gonna end up wid it? People like me? Hell no! It go in de bassmon's pockets, like always. De teacha . . . he all happy 'bout de hope fa de island . . . shit! . . . dere no hope fa dis island. It always be de same."

"Quit your bitchin'," said Mike. "There's sure as hell a better way to change it than drugs and killing people."

"Wa yu know? Yu live de life of luxury in de U.S.A. Yu don know dis island. Yu don know how de people live . . . wa de people feel. Yu know why we tek de drugs to de U.S.A.? 'Cause we can sell 'em . . . dat why. Yu got de same problem, bassmon. Don tink yu don. Now let me git in dat Goddamn hole!"

And with that, Andre grabbed a flashlight that was clipped to one of the backpacks and headed head first into the hole.

A voice came echoing back, "Okay! Dis flatten out to deh bigger space. Send down de stuff, den git yur asses down here!"

The all looked at each other and Jake had to smile and shake his head.

"Do as the bassmon says," and began handing his equipment down to Andre's outstretched hands.

CHAPTER 29

The tunnel, itself, came to a small cavern where someone could stand, slightly bent, and then proceeded downward to another cavern, which was higher and allowed a full-grown man to stand. The tunnel then went on, veering left and right, and after forty-five minutes of looking at all the walls and ceiling with flashlights as they proceeded, it came to an end. The walls of the tunnel changed as it descended from earth shored up with timbers to stone as the larger caverns were entered and ended in a large cavern of limestone where one could hear the surf pounding against it. Shining their lights, they found a smaller cavern off to the left and proceeded into it, moving loose rock, and came to what appeared to be an opening that had been overgrown with vegetation. Hacking their way through, they found themselves on a stretch of beach, facing the ocean.

Moving back to the cavern where the tunnel ended, they set up lights and photographed the ceiling, the walls, and the floor, the Professor downloading the photographs taken into his laptop, and James making entries into a notebook.

"Well, it looks like Morgan did have a passage to the beach, but there's no cuts in any other caverns off this main tunnel, except the one that goes to the beach . . . no entrances into a cave system. Sorry, Professor, but it looks like that map has some other meaning," Jake said as he moved around, looking at the various aspects of the cavern, and stopping and staring at the wall on his right. He then moved back to the group, shaking his head. "Like I said . . . I'm sorry, but this is a dead end."

"It can't be," said the Professor. "No other way Morgan could have moved a vast treasure from the northern end of the island south. Let alone being a physical impossibility, it surely would have been historically recorded, and the only historical record we have is Morgan sailing into Port Royal after the Panamanian raid and being welcomed as a hero, with only a very, very small amount of treasure."

"Pack up our gear," said Jake. "We'll go back to the hotel, take a look at the photos and the map and see what we can come up with. Somewhere, we're missing something, and we need to find it."

Mack whispered to Mike, "What are we going to find? There's nothing here."

"You don't understand, Mack. He's a legend, too. He does this all the time. He sees things a different way. If he thinks there's something missing, something's missing. And if there is, he won't stop until he finds it."

"Hope you're right," said Mack, "'cause I sure don't see it."

"Cooyah!" exclaimed Andre. "We be on de goose chase. Dere be shit here . . . nuttin' but de rocks. Dat old bastard pirate . . . he hid de treasa somwhe else a fool evybody wid dat map. Dat be de plan all along."

James spoke up.

"Watch what you say. If the Professor says that's what he did, that's what he did."

Andre faked a bow.

"Me sorry, teacha. Me sorry, boy, me insult deh bassmon . . . but yu both be full of shit."

And with that, he walked into the side cavern and out onto the beach.

Once they packed up all the lights and other gear, the Professor said, "Sorry, gentlemen. We should go by way of the beach. No sense trying to climb back up through the tunnel."

With the dispirited James trailing behind him, he exited the cavern.

"I feel sorry for the guy," said Mike, "but look around. There's nothing here."

"No, there's something," said Jake. "We just have to find it," and he headed out.

Mike turned to Mack and said, "See, what did I tell you?" and they followed.

CHAPTER 30

When they were all outside, the Professor got out his cell phone.

"I'll call the hotel and have them send a boat down to the beach. That way, we won't have to lug all this equipment back. I paid one of the attendants at the gift shop at Firefly to drive the Land Rover back to the hotel, and it should be waiting for us when we get there."

An hour later, they were back at the hotel.

"I thought . . .," said the Professor, walking through the parking lot. "The Land Rover isn't here," and he placed a call to the gift shop at Firefly to find out what time their driver had left.

"Yes, hello. This is Professor Dixon. I'm inquiring about our vehicle. What? That's impossible. Oh, no. No. Yes. Yes, tell them we're at the hotel. I'm terribly sorry. Yes. Yes. Thank you," and he hung up the phone and stared out at the sea, shaking his head.

"Professor, what's going on?" asked Jake.

"That young man from the gift shop . . . had just come out of the entrance to the estate on the back road when a vehicle pulled out in front of him and opened fire. When they saw the windows and glass wouldn't break, they hit it with a grenade. The car was destroyed and the young man was killed."

"Sons-a-bitches!" said Mack, throwing his gear down to the ground. "Murdering sons-a-bitches!"

"All right, we need to get to work," said Jake. "Let's get this stuff in the hotel. After everybody's had a chance to clean up, we'll meet for dinner. Then we're going to spend the night finding what we're missing."

Then he started walking ahead, never looking back.

"We have debts to repay," and he headed up the stairs to the hotel entrance, the others following behind.

CHAPTER 31

Dinner had been served and eaten when Damian Henry arrived in the upstairs room above the Muslim restaurant in Kingston.

Sitting at the table with two of his henchmen, was Fadhil Ahmad, his contact with ISIS. Fadhil had wiped his mouth with a napkin and threw it on his plate.

"We almost had them today. They were very lucky."

Damian didn't sit. He was pacing back and forth. Suddenly, he turned on Ahmad, inches from his face.

"Nah, yu fool. Yu be de lucky one. Dey be nah good to us dead, mon. Yu nah unnerstan. Me men wen down de hole afta dey lef. Dere nuttin' dere. It be a tunnel to de beach, nuttin' else. Dey naah find anyting yet. We donna waan kill dem. We waan use dem."

"I disagree," said Ahmad. "You tried scaring them with your little explosion, and it didn't work."

"Yu be de fool. Yu nah unnerstan. It work esactly as me waan. Yu donna know de Jake Sullivan. Me do. Wa me did only piss him off . . . mek him more intense. He naah stop now til he find de treasa, which he canna nah do if he be dead. Yu unnerstan? Listen, dis be me island. Me be de bassmon here. We do dis me way! Yu unnerstan!?"

And with that, he picked up a leg of mutton that was sitting on Ahmad's plate, took a bite, spit it out, and threw the mutton back on his plate.

"How yu people eat dis shit?" and he turned on his heel and walked out the door.

The men sitting with Ahmad asked what he wanted them to do.

"For now, nothing . . . but Mr. Henry's time will come. I will see to that myself. It is better if we let him think he is in charge, keeping his little secrets from me. But he is only another foolish infidel. I must speak with Ibrim."

Meanwhile, Damian headed for his car with his two subordinates, who had been right outside the door, guns ready, while he was arguing with Ahmad.

"Goddamn Arab bastards!" he said. "Dey smell like de shit dey eat!"

CHAPTER 32

It was a more subdued dinner that night on the veranda at the Casa Maria Hotel. Everyone was thinking, keeping to themselves, trying to figure out what they had missed. Jake could sense the tension.

"Well, anybody have anything?" he said.

"Sorry, Jake," said Mike. "Nothing."

"Same here," said Owens.

The Professor, who had been reviewing the photographs on his laptop, threw up his hands.

"I must admit my error. I can find nothing . . . no entrance into a cave system."

Jake took off the belt he was wearing and opened the zipper on the inside and took out the map. He opened it and studied it closely.

"All right. Let's think this through. This map, if it's the real thing, clearly shows a path from Port Maria south to an X. Professor, didn't you tell me when we left the airport that Port Royal was on the end of that spit of ground?"

"Yes, it's right at the entrance to the harbour."

"Odd . . . it says Port Royal, but the X is on the mainland, not on that spit of ground."

"I have a copy here," said the Professor, pulling it up on his computer. "Yes, you're right. I wonder . . ."

"What, Professor?"

"Nothing. I'm just thinking of something. I need to do a little investigation."

"But it doesn't change anything. The treasure still appears to have been moved from the north coast of the island to the south coast of the island, and based upon the topography that we saw on the drive up here, the Professor's right. There was no way to go over land. So, either Morgan found another method of moving the treasure along the path that was drawn on this map, or he took it into Port Royal by sea, somehow unobserved, which would have been almost impossible. And there's the clues – 'look out', a reference to the bluff at Firefly – 'follow the path', the tunnel down to the beach – if we do that, it leads to 'Satisfaction', Morgan's flagship, 'once lost', which it was, 'now found', which it would be if we found the treasure . . . at least what would have been its contents – 'lift me up and push on' and 'the riches of Sodom shall be yours'. And Professor, according to you, 'Sodom' is Port Royal."

"It has to be," said the Professor. "Too much of a coincidence to use that terminology and mean something else."

"So the line we don't have . . . the key to this whole thing . . . 'lift me up and push on.'"

"Wait a minute," said Mike, "where is Morgan buried?"

"'Lift me up' . . . dig up the body . . . you might be right," said Owens.

"Sorry gentlemen," said the Professor. "Captain Morgan was buried in a cemetery on that same spit of land in Port Royal. During the earthquake of 1692, the whole cemetery ended up in the Caribbean Sea."

Mike threw the map on the table.

"So there's another dead end."

The Professor was rubbing his eyes.

"James, have you come up with anything?"

"I'm sorry, Professor. I've studied those photographs and I can't find anything."

"Gentlemen, I'm going to retire," said the Professor. "Maybe we'll have better luck tomorrow."

"Yu get de rest teacha," said Andre. "Me pologise fa befo. Me still belief in yu . . . yu figure dis out. Yu see."

"I'm with you, Professor," said Mike. "It's been a long day."

"Me, too," said Mack. "What about you, Jake?"

"I'm going to sit here for a while. Professor, can I have your laptop? I'm going to look at those photographs one more time."

"Certainly," and he handed Jake the laptop.

"All right, gentlemen," said Jake, "I'll see you in the morning."

Mike yawned and pointed at Jake.

"Do your thing, will you? Discover the secret and let's get this over with."

Jake just smiled and began looked at photographs downloaded to the laptop.

He went over them time after time after time, ordering more coffee to stay awake. Finally, he saw it. On one of the photographs, the lights were situated in such a way that there was a shadow on the wall where there should not have been one, given the rock formations. He stared at it and saw that the shadow was caused by edges that looked like the fin of a shark, and there was a series of them. He looked back at the map and looked at the photograph and sat back. He went back over everything he had learned about the cave since the beginning, and then he looked at the photograph and the phrasing on the map one last time. He had it.

"Waves," he said. "They're waves."

He got on his cell phone and called Mike.

"Mike! Get up!"

"Come on, man, it's three o'clock in the morning. Don't you ever sleep?"

"Wake everybody up! I think I have the answer!"

"What?!" said Mike, now fully awake. "We'll be down in fifteen minutes."

Jake studied the photograph and the map once again. He was almost sure he was right. If he was, it was a remarkable feat of engineering . . . but it had to be.

Sargent Bennett had been kind enough to provide them with another Land Rover in which they had stowed all their gear before dinner, agreeing that the Shower Posse had added another murder to their long list, and it would probably remain unsolved for a lack of proof, as many of the others had. He was doing whatever he could with the contacts he had, but, unfortunately, the contacts and the informants for the Posse outweighed his own.

Finally, after fifteen minutes, the bleary-eyed crew arrived.

"This better be good, Jake," said Mack. "I was dreaming about a wonderful night in Miami."

"Please," said Mike, "no details. Way too early."

The Professor was wide awake.

"What is it? What did you find? How did you solve it?"

"Let me show you, Professor. Come on. Everybody in the car. Let's go."

So they all entered the vehicle, with James slowly rubbing the sleep out of his eyes and cleaning his glasses with his shirttail, Andre pushing him into the van.

They headed down the road to the beach, and once they were there, Jake gave directions.

"All we need is flashlights. We'll walk down the beach and enter through the cave entrance into the main cavern."

They did as they were told and twenty-five minutes later stood in the cavern, flashlights shining around.

Mike, yawning once again looked at Jake.

"All right. Come on. Do your thing."

Jake walked over to the wall, the pictures of which he had been staring at for most of the night.

"Professor, didn't you tell me that 'Morgan', in Old Welsh, meant 'of the sea'?"

"Yes, exactly. It does."

Jake stood off to the side and played his flashlight on the limestone wall.

"You see that?"

They all stared.

"Not really," said Mack. "What are you talking about?"

Jake went over and outlined with his fingers and said, "These," and moved his fingers along the raised edges. The Professor was staring as Jake did it, and then he took off his glasses, rubbed his eyes, and looked again.

"My God!" he said. "They're waves."

"Exactly . . . 'of the sea.'" Holding up the map, he said, "The clue we didn't understand – 'lift me up and push on,'" and with that, Jake put his hand at the bottom of the wave, feeling a small edge, and pushed up with all his might, but nothing happened.

He stood back and then bent down, this time, pushing, his strength coming from his legs and moving up his body, and the wave formation that had been so intricately carved into the limestone that it was almost invisible, moved as it slid up.

"And push on," said Jake, as he pushed the wave formation with all his might into the limestone wall, and then they heard the sound of metal moving, and a shower of dust and pebbles came down as a wave of cool air blew into the cavern, and slowly a here-to-fore invisible door opened in the side of the limestone wall.

Mike, yawning, slapped Jake on the back and said, "Jake Sullivan does it again."

Andre yelled, "Cooyah! See, teacha . . . yu be right all de time! Me Faada be right, too!" He thought, "De gift he give to me . . . it gwine mek all de difference in me life."

CHAPTER 33

Shining their flashlights on the entrance Jake had discovered, they pulled open the door just enough to allow them to pass through. They found themselves in a small cavern.

Just as they were panning around it with their lights, James screamed, "Professor!" and they all looked in the area that his light illuminated.

There sitting against the wall was a skeleton dressed in tattered rags, with only his buckled shoes and bandoleer intact. Protruding from his chest was what appeared to be a sword of some type, and Professor Dixon quickly went over and knelt down, took photographs, and examined the remains.

"So, Professor, who's our friend?" asked Owens.

Not responding, Dixon continued his examination. Finally, he rose and spoke to the group.

"If I had to bet, I'd say this was Captain Morgan's First Mate and most trusted underling . . . Bartholomew."

Shining his flashlight around the room, he saw there was a duplicate door to the one they had entered on the far side of the cavern.

"My guess is when we open that door, we'll be into the cave system that will lead us to Port Royal, and along the way, we'll find the bodies of those men who hauled the fortune from Panama to its last location. Morgan and Bartholomew probably overcame the group and killed them or buried them alive. Then when they had safely made their way back to the entrance, Morgan dispatched the last living individual who knew the location of his treasure, other than himself."

"Dat ting gimme de creeps," said Andre. "De bad juju."

Mike went over and looked at the skeleton.

"Nothing a first class pirate wouldn't do."

Jake, meanwhile, began examining the door that they had come through. It was a simple system. By pushing up on the wave-designed rock outside and then pushing in, it had lifted up a metal bar and pushed it away from the latch, allowing the door to swing open. He pushed the door shut and closed it, dropping the latch down into its bracket. The back of the door was wooden timbers with bolt heads throughout.

"What do you think of this, Professor?" asked Jake.

After examining the door, the Professor said, "My guess is they bore holes in pieces of limestone and then put bolts through the wood into those holes to make a façade on the outside of the wooden door. Chipping away at it and sanding it down, they were able to make the outside seem like one solid wall. Amazing when you think about it."

Then he turned.

"But now, it's time to see what's beyond the other door."

"You're right, Professor," said Mike as he walked over and lifted the latch on that door and pushed it out.

They were now in a tall cavern with no end in sight, with a large open area all around. As they played their flashlights around it, they were able to make out the far walls between hanging stalactites and rising stalagmites, except for one area where there was nothing but darkness. Professor Dixon shown his light in that direction.

"That's the way we go, gentlemen. Keep following the passages. Once I have my GPS transmitter, I'll be able to tell exactly where we are under the surface of the island as we make our way south."

"Think our pirate friends left markings?" asked Mack.

"My guess is they wouldn't," said Dixon. "I'm sure Morgan made his way back and forth several times and wouldn't want to take a chance that anyone would find the opening and follow. Not only that, when the time was right for his plan for joining Spain, and he wanted to come back through the cave system, he obviously knew the way."

"So, we're traveling blind," said Mike, "through all these caverns that might have side passages."

"We'll be all right," said the Professor. "We have the map, we know generally the direction we are going, and I've set the coordinates for our destination. We'll be all right."

"Well, one thing is certain," said Jake, "we've beaten Damian. This door hasn't been opened before, and without the map, he doesn't have the necessary clue. There's no way he's going to be able to follow us or track us any longer as we move through the cave system." He looked at Andre. "That's the trump card."

"It's late, gentlemen. My suggestion is since our vehicle is close by, we unload it and bring in our equipment and store it in this small chamber, go back to the hotel and get some sleep, and start out tomorrow after we've rested, had something to eat, and have our energy level back up where it will need to be."

"What kind of trek are we talking about?" asked Mike.

"It's approximately fifty miles from where we are to the destination point. If we can make three miles an hour, that would be normal walking time. Given that we're going through caves that might have impediments, I'm figuring two miles an hour. If we can walk for ten hours each day, that's twenty miles. So, I'm figuring it is going to take us two and a half days. Again, it will depend on the terrain, but hopefully we can keep up that pace."

Knowing his partner too well, Jake smiled and asked, "What do you think of that, Mike?"

"Just great," said Mike. "Just great. Can't wait to get started."

Owens slapped him on the back.

"It'll be fine, Mike. Just think . . . another adventure for you and Jake."

"Yeah," Mike muttered, "just what we need."

"All right," said Jake, "let's go get our gear and get it stored in here. Mike, since you're so anxious to get out, do me a favor. Go on the outside. I want to open this door and push it shut again. Look at it. See if there are any obvious cracks in the wall now that we've opened it that would let someone figure out that this door is here."

"Gladly," said Mike, as he lifted the latch, pulled open the door, and went back outside.

"Pull the wave design toward you, Mike. That should swing the door tight, and then push it down."

Mike did just that, the door moving easier than it had on its first opening, and when he had pushed the wave design down as far as it would go, he stood back with his flashlight and looked at the door. It was truly amazing. There were no seams visible the way the rock overlaid the entrance. He went back to the wall, pushed up the wave formation, and then pushed it in, and the door once again swung open.

"Can't see a thing from out here. We're good to go," said Mike.

They all came out, except Jake.

"All right, now here's what I'm gonna do. I'm going to pull this shut and close it from the inside. See if the seal is still good."

Completing the task and then opening the door to come out, Jake asked, "How was it?"

"Truly remarkable," said the Professor. "You can't see a thing. It's as if it's a sheer wall."

"Good," said Jake, "then our opening and closing of it isn't going to change anything, and Damian's never going to find it. Let's go get our gear in . . . now that we're definitely ahead of the game."

"Dat be good, bassmon," said Andre. "Damian deserve to lose. He nah gwine be de rich mon he tink. But he still gonna pay fa de sins. Me see to dat."

And with that, he headed outside.

CHAPTER 34

After two trips bringing all their gear into the cavern, making sure the doorway was secure, they worked their way back to the vehicle and then drove up the coast to the hotel.

Saying their goodnights, each of them headed to bed to get what rest they could. The euphoria of their discovery foretold a restless night for most.

It was several hours later when a phone rang. Slowly coming out of a deep sleep, Damian Henry reached for his cell.

"Who dis?" he said, and then he heard the words that put a huge smile on his face. "Excellent. Yu do dis job well. Keep in touch. When de treasa be found, den we mek our move. Naah worry 'bout dat. Do wa me say. It be arright," and he clicked off the phone and lie there, looking at the ceiling, still smiling, thinking that Morgan's treasure would soon be his.

CHAPTER 35

They assembled mid-morning and had a hearty breakfast on the balcony.

"Gentlemen," said the Professor, "this is our last big meal for a while. From now on, it's going to be power bars, Gatorade, and water for the next several days."

After finishing their meal, they had one of the attendants at the hotel take them to the beach where they had parked the previous night, their story being that they were going on a hike along the beach and doing some sightseeing in some of the other towns along the coast.

The Professor slipped the driver some money and told him, "Charles, if we're not back in the next few nights, don't worry. We may take a cab to some of the night spots in Ocho Rios," he said, winking at the driver, who smiled, knowingly.

"Nanna problem, Professor. We hold de rooms. Yu com back when yu waan."

"Thank you, Charles. I appreciate it," said the Professor.

The group watched as Charles turned the Land Rover around and headed back to the hotel.

"Nice going, Professor," said Mike. "That should keep anyone from wondering about where we are."

"I hope so," said the Professor. "That was the idea."

They entered the cavern from the beach, as before, opened the latch mechanism, and entered the smaller chamber where their equipment had been stored for the night, pulling the door shut behind them and making sure it was securely latched.

They then opened the secondary door and moved into the larger cavern, shutting the door behind them, using the same carved system to secure the latch on that door from the outside.

Their flashlights in hand and backpacks on, carrying their equipment and necessities, they were ready to move out. The Professor took one more look at the place where they had just exited through the limestone wall.

"It truly is genius," said the Professor, "what they were able to do three hundred years ago. If someone was exploring these caves, they never would have found the entranceway to that chamber from either side. Henry Morgan was an amazing man," he said shaking his head. Then, turning to the group, he said, "Gentlemen, if I am correct, this cavern is the beginning of a whole group of caves connected to each other all along the foothills of the Blue Mountains and will move southward, and . . . if Morgan's map is to be believed, end up somewhere near Port Royal. Shall we begin?"

"Yu be de bass, teacha," said Andre. "Lead de way."

And with that, they headed into the caves.

CHAPTER 36

Thanks to the efforts of President Fletcher's team, the GPS transmitter was working flawlessly as they progressed through the caverns, beholding amazing sights of stalactites and stalagmites and limestone formations.

Their travels took them through narrow passages where they had to stoop over and into large, cathedral-like caverns, that were awe-inspiring in their beauty and grandeur.

They crossed small streams flowing through the caves, waved off the occasional bat, and moved in an eerie silence, the only sound their feet and equipment as it came in contact with the stone surface.

They were able to make steady progress, stopping briefly after every hour or so, to drink and rest. They made their way steadily south. The Professor had been right . . . there were no markings . . . but when they would come to a cavern with side tunnels, Professor Dixon would stop and check their coordinates on his GPS transmitter to make sure of their location under the surface of Jamaica, and he would not hesitate to lead them in the direction it indicated led to their destination.

They had just made a stop to rest in a large cavern with side tunnels and Professor Dixon was doing his calculations, when Andre stood up and looked around.

"Whe de boy? Whe dat James be?"

The Professor looked up and looked around him.

"I don't know."

"I'm here, Professor," said James, his flashlight beam shining from the direction from which they had just come. "There was an amazing stalagmite formation on the floor back in that chamber. I wanted to make some limestone carvings," and he held up a small bag. "I think it would be interesting to date these as we go, Professor."

The Professor chuckled, "Good thinking, James. Keep up the good work."

James smiled, but Andre did not, and he gave James a long, hard look as he passed by him.

They moved on and finally came to a cavern with various rock formations that only went two or three feet off the ground and ended in a shelf-like plateau when the Professor announced, "Gentlemen, we've been on the move for close to ten hours, and we've done better than expected. By my calculations, we've traversed twenty-five miles of our journey, and if we can do this tomorrow, we'll reach our destination."

"Twenty-five miles . . ." said Mike, "Gee, it only seems like twenty," as he collapsed on one of the plateaus, throwing his backpack down beside him.

"All right, we'll spend the night here, gentlemen," said Jake.

They unloaded their sleeping bags, passed out the power bars, Gatorade, and water and sat and talked. Also, as they sat, Mike, Owens, and Jake checked their weapons, having come on the expedition fully armed, knowing that they might have an encounter with members of the Shower Posse cartel. They all wore ankle sheaths with knives and back holsters with Glock 17s. Owens also had a separate ankle holster.

"Thank goodness those haven't been necessary," said the Professor.

"Not yet, anyway," said Owens, "but we still don't know how this is going to play out."

"Well, we can only hope," said Mike, "that Jake's right, and the bad guys don't know we're here. And with that, gentlemen, I'm going to get some sleep."

Mike laid out his sleeping bag on the ledge, crawled in, and rolled over, facing the rock. The others followed suit, leaving only a small battery-powered lantern aglow in the middle of the cavern floor.

CHAPTER 37

Another meeting in the rooms above the Muslim restaurant was taking place. Fadhil was furious.

"My men have searched the cavern again and again! There are no signs of them! The fool at the hotel that drove them to the beach said they headed north." Pacing as he talked, he speculated. "Morgan probably came to the north shore of the island and then unloaded his plunder and hid it in one of the caves along the coast, and the map has led them to it. And we have no idea where they are. I told you that we should have struck! Taken them hostage and made them talk before we killed them!"

Damian sat stone-faced, relaxing in a chair, as Ahmad continued his rant.

"You do know what'll happen to you if we don't find this treasure, don't you?" asked Ahmad.

"Do me look worried?" asked Damian. "Tek it easy. It be arright. Damian know esactly whe dey be, a when de time is right, de treasa will be mine . . . a den we mek our deal a it be yurs . . . but me told yu befo, dis be me island. Me run de show." He sat back and smiled smugly. "Me hab it all unda de control."

Ahmad walked up to where he was sitting and glared at him.

"You better be correct, Mr. Henry. You better have everything under control, or by Allah, you will wish we had never met!" and he stormed out of the room.

Damian looked up at one of his associates.

"Dese Arab bastards . . . me arredy wish we neba met," and checked the time on his thirty thousand dollar Rolex Submariner, knowing that soon he should be receiving another call.

CHAPTER 38

Ahmad sat in his vehicle, also waiting for a call.

"Why do you let that infidel pig speak to you in such a fashion, excellency?" asked his driver.

"My fake rage was to see if he was still calm, still in control, and to assure him his knowledge was still shared with no one. He will continue to do our work for us, but when the treasure is found, we will know, and Mr. Henry will make payment."

Just then, his cell rang.

"Ah, good. Just in time. Report to me, Ibrim . . ."

CHAPTER 39

Jake didn't know whether he had been dreaming or had actually heard a noise, but as he looked around the cavern, he could see that Mike, Owens, and the Professor were sleeping soundly while Andre was tossing on the ledge where he slept.

Then Jake realized that James was gone. Jake lie back down, rolled onto his side, and waited, pretending to be asleep. Soon James came back into the chamber from the direction from which they had come and lie down, rolled over, and was soon asleep. Jake, too, rolled over.

"Bathroom break," he thought, as, soon, he was once again asleep.

CHAPTER 40

After several hours rest, the Professor had them up and moving again through the caves from one cavern to another, as he constantly checked his GPS to make sure they were headed in the right direction.

They made good time, keeping a steady pace, but seeing that everyone was tiring, Jake stopped them for a break.

"How much farther do we have to go, Professor?" asked Mike.

The Professor looked up and smiled.

"If I'm correct and we don't encounter any obstacles, another leg like we just completed should bring us within only a few hours from our destination."

With that, Mike stood up and strapped his pack back on.

"I'm tired of being underground. Let's get moving and find this treasure so we can see sunlight again."

"I'm with you," said Mack.

Andre and the Professor were also on their feet, ready to go.

Sensing the determination of the group, Jake also rose.

"All right. We're all in agreement. Let's get this done."

CHAPTER 41

The Professor had been pretty close. They had come through a smaller chamber, where they had to double over again to make it through, and then exited into one of the larger caverns they had encountered. They swung their lights all around. There was no exit.

"Looks like we've come to the end of the line," said Mack. "No treasure chests . . . and no way out."

"No," said the Professor, "it has to be here, if I'm right, it has to be here somewhere."

"What are you talking about, Professor?" asked Jake. "Where exactly are we?"

"Do you remember on the map?" asked the Professor. "Remember you stating that on Morgan's map the X marking the location of the treasure was on the mainland, not actually on the Palisadoes where Port Royal was located?"

"I do," said Jake, "and . . .?"

"There was always a legend that the many forts of Port Royal that were constructed by the British along the entrance to the harbour were all connected by underground tunnels to provide access for troop movements and supplies in case of a siege. Although Fort Charles was the main fort, there were forts all over the harbour area . . . Fort Nugent, Fort Clarence, Fort Augusta, and many others.

When I looked at the X on the map and translated it into a GPS position, it appeared the X sat directly on top of Passage Fort, which guarded the Rio Cobre, the waterway into the mainland. It was constructed by the Spanish to guard the route to St. Jagode la Vega, now known as Spanish Town, and was the fort the British captured when they took control of the island in 1655.

We know it was still in existence in the late 1600s under the command of a Colonel Doyly, based upon the historical record.

So, I ask for your faith once again, gentlemen. We need to check these walls thoroughly. Somewhere, I believe there is a tunnel, probably sealed off by Morgan and Bartholomew, that lies deep beneath the harbour's waters and leads to the location of the treasure at Port Royal."

They all looked at each other, and finally, Andre was the one who spoke.

"Teacha . . . he naah be wrong yet. Me go check de walls."

"Andre's right," said Owens. "Let's go."

And with that, they all began to see if they could find anything that appeared to be an opening.

Finally, from behind an outcropping, Mike said, "This isn't a natural formation. These rocks were placed here by hand."

He began taking them down. Everyone stopped looking around immediately and put down their gear to go over and help him. They set up a floodlight to shine on the area. Once they had enough rocks down where they could see, Mike used a flashlight to see what lay beyond and recoiled at what he saw.

"The Professor was right," said Mike. "Morgan made sure his secret was safe. The boys in there look a lot like Bartholomew."

"So, it looks like we found the Professor's tunnel," said Mack.

"Come on," said the Professor, "let's get the rest of these rocks out of the way," and they set up a firemen's carry to clear the entrance.

CHAPTER 42

Mike had been right. Ten skeletons in tattered clothes, only the leather on them surviving intact, lined one wall of the tunnel . . . some facing down, some facing up, and some on their backs. The Professor examined each and then stood up to report his findings.

"At least they weren't buried alive," he said. "There's a round hole in each skull . . . probably from a round mini ball from a flintlock pistol."

"Why would they just accept it?" asked Mike. "Why wouldn't they fight back?"

Without answering, the Professor went to a pile of rags that had once been a sack and moved around some pots and held up what appeared to be a clay jug and a vile to his flashlight and smelled inside both.

"I told you . . . Morgan was a brilliant tactician. He knew they were exhausted, but he made sure. This vile contained valerian, a strong sedative of the era, which he used to lace this jug of rum before passing it out to his men to celebrate their accomplishments. Little did they know that celebration would be the last thing they enjoyed in this life. Morgan was making sure his secret was staying here."

His excitement growing, the Professor looked at his watch, knowing they were close.

"We best be moving on," he said, and began walking through the tunnel that had been honed through the limestone and went steadily downhill under the Caribbean, heading to the then bustling sea port of Port Royal.

CHAPTER 43

The tunnel finally opened into a large cavern. Playing their flashlight beams around them in an arc, it appeared there was no exit other than the way they had come in. They began to separate and move about. Jake went around a small outcropping of rock, his flashlight playing off the walls, when he saw it.

He was not quite sure what they were at first, so he moved closer. Stairs . . . wooden stairs . . . going up the wall of the cavern . . . and then he looked up and set into the ceiling above him was what appeared to be a wooden door – an old fashioned trap door. Then, looking to his left, he saw the wooden beam and realized he was looking at a handmade hoist. He saw the metal hook at the end of a rope and saw the platform on the ground with the ropes laying on it all connected to a metal ring. He could just imagine them working, loading the treasure chests onto the platform, and then using the winch and pulley system, to lift the platform up and swing it over to the trap door where the chests would be unloaded into whatever was above them.

"Over here!" he cried.

They came toward him and looked around in awe, thinking of how remarkable it was what men could do with simple tools, what they could create with will power, hard work, and imagination, knowing deep down inside that above them could be one of the richest treasures ever discovered.

While the floodlights were set up to illuminate the entire cavern, Jake continued walking about and came to a far wall of limestone. Looking down at his feet, he realized that he was standing in a puddle of water. Playing his light along the wall, he could see cracks in the limestone with small rivulets of water running down from those cracks.

"Professor!" he called out. "Come here a minute!"

Once again, the group turned and followed.

"This isn't a problem, is it?" he asked, as his light played over the water.

Examining the limestone walls, Professor Dixon said, "No, this seepage has occurred over centuries. You have to understand that this area has seen its share of earthquakes, including the great one of 1692, but this cavern has been here for over three hundred years, and the Caribbean has not been able to penetrate it yet. So, hopefully, these walls will still be here long after we have completed our task."

"I don't understand something," said Mike. "You told us about that earthquake before, Professor, and I thought everything slid down into the sea when the sand became liquefied. But Morgan did all this before the earthquake. How is that trap door going to lead to a warehouse when that warehouse was moved by the earthquake twenty years after Morgan was here?"

"Good question, Mr. Lang," said the Professor. "The answer is it didn't move. Let me explain. It's obvious that what we see in this cavern was created by Morgan and his men before the raid on Panama in 1671.

I can only tell you what I believe to be true, based upon what I observe and what history tells us about the earthquake. I believe that Morgan reached this cavern and knew he was at the end of the system . . . there was nowhere else to go. Having come through the tunnel, he believed himself to be under Port Royal, and he was correct. His men chipped this opening through the roof of this cavern, and my guess is when they finally reached daylight, they were somewhere in the old wharf area of Port Royal. At that point, Morgan would have covered his tracks and hid the opening until he could construct a warehouse on top of the site. That warehouse would rest not on sand, as many of the other buildings did in Port Royal, but on the top of this limestone cavern.

When the earthquake of 1692 struck and the sand was liquefied by the vast amount of water seeping through the surface of the earth, the foundations of the buildings would have crumbled, they would have collapsed inward, and the ruins would have slid into the Caribbean.

Although there has only started to be explorations of that part of Port Royal which lies under the sea, from those explorations, we know that is the condition of many of the buildings that were covered during the earthquake.

However, we also know that prior to the earthquake of 1907, there were writings that indicated you could float along the surface above the sunken city of Port Royal and see the rooftops of sunken buildings. After that earthquake, the buildings and debris dropped even lower and many of the buildings that once could be seen could no longer be seen. However, again, this cavern did not drop lower, and because the warehouse of Henry Morgan sat on top, it did not sink any further. The years of sediment, sea growth, and sand simply covered the warehouse roof and obscured it from view over all these centuries.

The one thing I cannot tell you, Mr. Lang, unfortunately, is the condition of the interior of that warehouse. Obviously, it is sitting below the surface of the Caribbean Sea, and its condition would depend upon the steps that Morgan took to ensure its integrity and security."

"What do you mean, Professor?" asked Owens.

"If I was Henry Morgan," said the Professor, "I would have built that building out of block and brick, with no windows and no doors, making this trap door the only entrance.

After all the effort we have seen Morgan go through to ensure that no one knew the route to that warehouse, it only makes sense to me that he would want that trap door to be the only means of getting into it. If that's the case and it's well built, it could well have withstood the ravages of the sea for the past three centuries and still be intact."

"Okay," said Mike. "Time to go find the treasure," and he headed toward the wooden steps, quickly climbing up.

He was almost to the first landing when the riser on which he had just put his weight collapsed beneath him and he began to fall. Grabbing hold of the railing and fighting to gain purchase with his feet, he righted himself and crawled onto the landing and sat there for a moment to catch his breath and regain his composure.

"Be careful, Mr. Lang!" yelled the Professor. "That wood has been sitting there for three hundred years. It's bound to have rotted away in some places."

"You think?" replied Mike. "Thanks for the warning, Professor."

The Professor turned to Jake and said, "I suppose I should have told him sooner."

Jake just laughed and said, "Don't worry. He'll be all right. Come on, Mike! This isn't recess! Let's go!"

"Come on, Mike, let's go," Mike muttered under his breath as he headed up the steps to the next landing, right beneath the trap door, this time moving much slower and much more carefully, trying to stay on the edges of the risers where his weight would find its support.

The trap door was secured with a padlock, and Mike took out his Glock and pounded at it with the butt of the weapon, until finally he was able to pull the hasp out of the semi-rotten wood. He pushed against the trap door with his shoulder, but it wouldn't budge. Squatting down, he used the strength of his legs and rose up, his shoulder again pressing against the door, and he could finally feel some movement. Continuing to press as hard as he could, the door finally gave way, and he was able to swing it open and hoist himself up and disappeared from view.

"Mike!" hollered Jake, "what's up there?"

A few minutes passed, and then Mike's head appeared in the opening.

"You're not going to believe it," said Mike. "Allow me to introduce you to the lost treasure of Henry Morgan."

"Cooyah!" yelled Andre. "Me tell yu de Professor know his shit! He be de bassmon," and he walked up and hugged the Professor. "Way to go, teacha! Yu be de mon!"

"Congratulations, Professor. Nice job," said Jake.

Mack smiled and shook the Professor's hand.

"I have to get up there and see this with my own eyes," said Dixon, as he started to move toward the stairs going up the wall.

CHAPTER 44

"Stop right there Professor!" came a voice from the other side of the cavern.

They all turned. There stood James . . . holding an automatic weapon.

"Mr. Lang, throw your weapon down here, please!"

Mike hesitated.

"Do it now, Mr. Lang, or I'm afraid this celebration is going to be short-lived."

Mike did so, and at that moment, Mack Owens reached for his weapon. James caught the movement out of the corner of his eye and swiveled and fired, the burst from the automatic weapon catching Mack in his right shoulder, and he went down.

"All right!" yelled Jake. "Enough! Enough!"

"Not yet, Mr. Sullivan. Owens, throw out your weapon."

With his left hand, Owens reached across him, took it out of his right hand, and threw it down on the floor of the cavern close to where Jake was standing.

"I'm not going to let him bleed to death," said Jake. "Let me get over there."

James motioned him over with the weapon, and Jake ran to Mack's side. Jake yelled, "Professor, give me the first aid kit out of the backpack!"

"Easy!" yelled James. "Very slowly. I don't want to see anything come out of that bag but the first aid kit."

"James," said Dixon, "what are you doing? What's wrong with you?"

"There's nothing wrong with me, Professor."

And then Mike spoke up from above.

"How long ago did ISIS recruit you?"

Professor Dixon looked at Mike in shock and exclaimed, "No! It can't be!"

"Oh, yes it can be . . . and it is. It was after I began working for the Professor, Mr. Lang. It was his constant teaching about the history of this island that led me to start thinking on my own. I slowly grew to despise the colonials, who'd used Jamaica and all the other islands of the Caribbean to create their own wealth . . . to make the rich richer . . . to promote the economy of the West India Company . . . and all the other businesses that grew and thrived on the backs of slavery and misery in these islands. And then I found the website . . . that led me to the Koran, and I converted to Islam. You see, ISIS is doing exactly what is needed. The countries in the west, the United States, Europe, parts of Asia, such as Russia, China, and Japan, all thrive on the backs of the downtrodden. The rich get richer and the poor get poorer, and the governments don't really give a damn. We need a revolution, but those governments are so entrenched and the people are so numb to their condition that they will never rise up against their oppressors, but ISIS will lead a holy war against all the infidels. They will strike at the heart of capitalism all over the world and bring these nations to their knees . . . and after, with the blessings of Allah, a new world order will arise . . . one based on equality and the blessings provided by Him."

"James, how could you?" asked the Professor. "How could you belong to such a group? They're not saviors. They're terrorists and murderers! They commit acts of despicable violence . . . not against the monied elite, but against children of the poor, cutting off the heads of those who won't join their cause!"

"Professor, you have studied history. And, please call me by my Muslim name . . . Ibrim Abd al Hakim. I chose it in your honor, Professor. It means 'servant of the wise'. You know that great changes in society need some spilling of blood . . . and once the goal is realized, the bloodletting stops and peace reigns supreme. Professor, it's right in front of you . . . don't you see? They're all alike . . . the monied, the privileged . . . it's their whole history. Don't you remember those men in the cavern? The wealthy and powerful Henry Morgan wanting to make more wealth and become more powerful . . . killing his own crew just to keep them quiet. Power always initially comes from hurt and fear and the will of Allah."

The Professor was furious.

"You're a coward and a murderer! You blaspheme by even mentioning Allah! You're nothing but butchers, and you'll never win!"

"Oh, we will, Professor. We will win. You still with us, Mr. Owens? You know what's going to happen, don't you? You've been with the DEA long enough to know how this plays out. This money is turned over to us by the Shower Posse, and we guarantee to protect their distribution routes and flood the market with pure Afghan heroin. We will have a base in Jamaica, and as we work into the Posse with each drug shipment that moves into the United States, we'll move one of our agents to indoctrinate the young of your country to get as many as we can hooked on such a powerful and debilitating narcotic. They will be poor and desperate, and they will be ours. We will teach them how they are kept that way by those in power, and they will become our agents, and they will bring daily attacks against your country. We will have our own army within the United States, striking at will at any time, and you will never know who they are, and you will never know when it's going to happen, and you will never stop it. Jamaica will become our base of operations in this hemisphere, and we will spread our beliefs and the word of Allah to South America, North America, Central America, Mexico, Canada, Bolivia, and Argentina. We will teach the young people everywhere to rise up against their oppressors and strike, and we will fuel it all with a simple white powder. We now control the poppy fields of Afghanistan, where your soldiers bled and died for a worthless cause. We will prove the end of you. Ask Mr. Owens. He knows it can happen."

"Now," he said, holding up what appeared to be a satellite phone, "I suggest you all sit down. The wait won't be long. You see, when my brethren learned of Damian's desire to become our sole agent for drug distribution, and he thought the way to obtain that status was through acquiring the legendary fortune of Henry Morgan as is described in the Professor's writings, it was simple for me to go to Damian and profess my allegiance to the Shower Posse, expressing my contempt for Professor Dixon and everything he stood for. I was very convincing, and Damian agreed that I would tag along on this expedition as his eyes and ears," he said, shaking the phone. "Naturally, everything I have reported to him, I have reported to my superiors. You see, they don't trust Damian Henry. They see him as a thieving, lying, infidel who will do anything to increase his own wealth and accumulate more power. They're satisfied with letting him do the work for them, and as you can see, hopefully," pointing to the ceiling, "we're only one step away from success, but ISIS had no intention of letting Damian conduct his search without it being monitored by them. So, gentlemen, I serve two masters . . . the Shower Posse cartel and ISIS . . . and I have notified them both every step of the way of our discoveries, and that first night, after we discovered the entrance to the cave, I made the necessary calls, and as we started through the caves, Damian Henry's men entered through that same door and have been lagging behind us, ready to attack at my signal.

Professor, you will see, we are not butchers . . . we are not heartless. Your deaths will be quick, and I will even consider your academic curiosity. I promise you won't be killed until you see the last of Morgan's plunder leave this cavern in the hands of the Shower Posse, soon to be transferred to ISIS, to ensure that our plans succeed."

CHAPTER 45

"I've got to prop up this shoulder."

James swung the automatic weapon again in Owens' direction.

"No tricks, Mr. Owens, or both you and Mr. Sullivan die."

"Jake, help me. Get under my one arm here."

Jake did as Owens asked, and when he did, his ear was close to Owens' mouth.

"Ankle holster, right leg," whispered Owens.

Jake squeezed his wrist where he was holding it, acknowledging that he understood, and helped Mack shift his weight to his other hip so he could lean his injured shoulder against the limestone.

In the movement, Mack's right leg went under his left.

"Jake, straighten out my leg. I've got a cramp that's killing me. Just straighten it out."

Jake looked at James and then raised his hands as if to ask if it was all right. James nodded.

"Careful, Mr. Sullivan."

Jake took Mack's right leg, and as he brought it out from under his left, he withdrew the .38 from the ankle holster, rolled quickly to his left, and came up firing. Caught off balance by the quick movement, James was too slow as he swiveled the automatic weapon in Jake's direction, and the bullets ricocheted off a rock outcropping. But Jake's found their mark. Three shots to the chest, and James went down. Jake walked over, picked up the Tec-9 and a bag holding several clips, and looked down at James. The Professor came over, also.

"What a tragedy. He could have done so much good in the world."

"We choose our paths, Professor," said Jake. "The path he chose is what led him here."

CHAPTER 46

After looking at his watch, Damian spoke to his subordinates.

"He mek de call by now. Somting's wrong."

"Bass, dey be in de caves. Meebe de call canna git through," said one of his men.

"Meebe," said Damian, and then walked out on the balcony of his estate and then walked back in. "But me gut tell me somting be wrong. Give de men de signal. Tell dem to move in on Andre a his friends. Evybody die 'cept de Professor. Him me need to find me treasa. Now move!"

The GPS towers President Fletcher had erected at the Professor's request not only worked for his GPS transmitter, but also for cell phones once they could be entered into the system. James had performed his duties well, and Damian's lieutenant had no trouble contacting the men in the tunnel, who had been lagging behind the group in front of them, but who now were on the attack.

CHAPTER 47

Just then, noises were coming from the caverns behind them . . . then shouting . . . the Shower Posse had arrived.

"Andre!" hollered Jake, "get Mack behind one of those rock formations! Can you still shoot, Mack?" he asked, holding up the weapon he had taken from his ankle holster.

"Don't worry, I'll be fine," said Mack, Andre catching the weapon as Jake tossed it.

Mike took cover behind the railings on the landing, and Andre made sure the Professor was safe behind one of the large stalagmites, and then he hollered over to Jake, "Jake Sullivan! Git me de gun! Me help yu!"

"Careful, Jake!" yelled Mack. "He's still Shower Posse!"

"Not wid dem! Me wid yu!"

Their attackers were in the cavern, firing their weapons and taking up positions. Jake looked at Andre long and hard in between firing rounds back at the attackers, and then he made a decision. He put a full clip in his Glock and threw it to Andre, as he switched to James' Tec-9.

The firefight continued for several minutes. Jake, Mack, and Andre returning fire, but the rock formations protecting them also protected the enemy. The targets were hard to find. The attackers had the advantage of manpower, as more and more entered the cavern and took up positions, trying to encircle them.

Mike hollered down, "We can't hold 'em off! There's too many of 'em!"

Jake knew he was right, but also knew they were trapped, and the only thing they could do was stand and fight.

"Professor, you all right?" he called to Dixon, crouched in fear behind another stalagmite. "Can you work that laptop?"

"I think so," said Dixon.

"Send Signal 3, now!"

Dixon opened the laptop and entered a code and then pressed send.

"Done!" said Dixon.

"All right, now Mack and I are going to give you cover. Andre, get the Professor and get him up to Mike."

"You can't come up here," said Mike. "We'll be trapped! This room up here has no doors or windows!"

"Do what I tell you!" yelled Jake. "Get the Professor up there!"

Andre fired off several rounds, ran to the Professor's position, helped him up, and headed for the steps.

"All right, Mack! Give 'em what you got!" and he and Owens began firing repeatedly toward the cavern entrance, their attackers firing back. Jake looked as Andre had the Professor on the landing by Mike. "Mike . . . get them up in the room! All right, Mack . . . you're next . . . go!"

"I'm not leaving you here."

"I know what I'm doing! Go!"

Reluctantly, Mack fired several more shots, looked at Jake, who smiled and nodded, and Mack, holding his shoulder, ran for the steps. Jake continued to fire, having grabbed an extra clip from James' backpack, lying at his feet. He saw that Mack made his way to the top and Mike was helping him up into the warehouse.

"Get him up in the room, Mike!" yelled Jake. When he saw that Mack was gone, he yelled at Mike again, "You're next! Get up there!"

"No way!" said Mike. "I'm not leaving you here alone."

Jake knew he could never talk Mike into leaving him there. He kept firing at the entrance until the clip was empty and then inserted a new one. Shots were coming at him from a different direction now, and he knew that Damian's men were circling around to surround him. He moved through the stalagmites until he was close to the wall where they had felt the water seeping through, and with his back to the stalagmite, braced himself and opened fire, putting round after round into the cavern wall where the water had been coming through small fissures.

Jake kept firing until the clip was empty, then threw down the weapon and sprinted to the stairs. Not worrying about the rotten wood, he climbed as quickly as possible to the first landing and stopped, bullets still whizzing around him.

"Come on, come on," he said, under his breath.

Mike hollered, "Jake! Get up here!"

"Come on . . . it has to work," said Jake, and then he heard a cracking, growing louder, and then there were water spouts coming through the cavern wall, and then they started to blow through . . . large holes . . . bursts of water, reaching the whole way to the tunnel . . . and then the entire wall collapsed inward and the Caribbean Sea roared into the cavern. Jake laughed as the water was almost at his feet.

"Jake, quit laughing like an idiot and get up here!" said Mike. He could now hear screaming as the water slammed into their attackers and drove them backwards into the cavern and went roaring down the tunnel, back toward Passage Fort.

Jake had sprinted up the risers to the top landing, racing ahead of the water, which was destroying the steps behind him. The landing was starting to shake as Jake reached it.

Mike sent him up into the room with one shove, lifting himself up behind him, rolling over and slamming shut the trap door, just as the sea rushed against it.

"This door's never going to hold back all that water," said Mike, kneeling and pushing against it with all his might.

"It'll be all right," said the Professor, coming up to him and putting his hand on his shoulder. "It'll be all right. Now that the cavern's almost full, the water pressure will flow out through the caves, filling them."

He was right. The door held.

CHAPTER 48

They all sat there, backs against the wall, catching their breath.

"Mack, let me take a look at that shoulder," said Mike, picking up the flashlight he had left in the room and removing the bandage where the bleeding had resumed, and used a piece of his shirt to bind the wound. "You're lucky. It just nicked you. There's no bullet in your arm. It'll hurt like hell, but you'll be all right."

"Thanks," said Mack. "I appreciate it."

Andre was standing there and had his flashlight on, sending it around the room.

"Me canna belief dis. De whole ting be true. De papas me give to yu, teacha. It all be true. Me Fadda be proud."

The rest had lost their flashlights in the melee below, so they followed Andre's as it panned around the room, as Mike added his to the illumination. There was chest after chest piled along all the walls, almost up to the ceiling, which appeared to be approximately eight feet high, and there were rough-cut pallets laden with "la plata" – the silver plate made from Incan treasure.

Andre walked over and opened the lid on one of the chests, and with the hinges rusted, it came free in his hand, revealing a chest full of pieces of eight, jewels, and golden artifacts.

"Cooyah!" he exclaimed. "De Morgan pirate treasa!"

"I can't believe it," murmured the Professor. "We actually found it."

Jake nodded.

"You found it, Professor. We were all just along for the ride."

Andre walked over to the Professor and extended his hand.

"All de people of dis island . . . dey be proud of yu."

The Professor extended his hand.

"Thank you, Andre. Thank you very much."

"I hate to break up the party," said Mike, playing his flashlight as he walked around the room, "but it appears that we are trapped, with the sea all around us and no way out of here."

Jake looked at the Professor.

"I take it your laptop didn't make it."

"Sorry, Mr. Sullivan."

"Don't worry. You sent the signal."

"Exactly what signal have you been talking about, Jake?" asked Mike.

"Something I worked out with Bates," said Jake. "He . . ." and he stopped in mid-sentence, as they all felt the room begin to shift, treasure chests sliding across the floor as the room tilted more and more to the right.

"What the hell!" said Owens.

"It's the cavern," said the Professor, standing up. "It must be collapsing in on itself. The loss of the outside wall put too much stress on the ceiling. The right side is caving in and it's slowly moving toward the left."

"Does that mean what I think it does?" asked Mike.

"I'm afraid so. This room is going to keep tipping to the right, until the stress is too much, and then the walls are going to give."

The Professor's words proved prophetic as soon as they were uttered, as a part of the wall on the right-hand side of the store room gave way with a loud crash, block being pushed in by the force of the sea as it rushed into the room.

"Try and get up to the high side," said Jake, pushing everyone to his left, but they were fighting a losing battle. The sea was too powerful.

"All we can do," yelled the Professor, "is wait until the water is near the top! That will lower the pressure, and we can swim out through the opening. As soon as we're out, head up. We should only be about twenty feet under water, and we should be able to hold our breath that long."

The water was up to their chests now, the room filling quickly as the building continued to tilt to its right . . . and that's when they saw the light coming in through the hole, and the first spear whizzed through the water, striking Professor Dixon in the thigh.

CHAPTER 49

Damian wasn't taking any chances. Once James had told him the destination was Port Royal, he had taken some of the boats the Posse owned and had them running back and forth in the channel that covered the sunken city. He had received the call that a large whirlpool had formed in the channel, and it looked like water was rushing somewhere beneath the sea. He immediately had ordered his divers in, and they were now coming through the opening created in the sunken warehouse.

"No choice!" yelled Mike to Jake. "Fight or drown! Give your knife to Andre! Help the Professor and Mack! Follow Andre and me . . . we'll make a path for you! You ready Andre?"

"Let's do dis, mon!"

And with that, Andre took Jake's knife and went below the surface, Mike following him.

Jake yelled to Mack and the Professor, "Hold your breath! Here we go!" and they, too, slipped beneath the surface as the room filled to the ceiling.

Andre went down low and saw a shadow above him and kicked up, his knife held ahead of him, and he thrust it into the midsection of the diver he made contact with. Dropping the knife and grabbing his spear gun, he dodged the spear from another attacker and fired back, hitting him in the shoulder. He saw Mike off to his left wrestling with another attacker and Jake pulling the Professor and Mack, coming up behind them.

He saw the lights of at least three more attackers coming toward them and knew it was a losing battle. As he hurried to Mike's aid, he pulled the mask off of the attacker as Mike sliced upward with his knife. They took off the attacker's tank and both took in air from the breathing device before heading to help Jake with Mack and the Professor.

The sea was clear and they were easy to spot, also making them easy targets for their attackers.

Mike passed the tank to Jake, who refused it and gave it to the Professor and then Mack, and then took some air. Mike pointed ahead to where the lights from even more attackers were coming, and he and Jake looked at each other, knowing they were about to make their last stand.

Mike pointed down, and he and Andre were ready to dive down and come up underneath the attackers as they had before, when Mike stopped him and pointed. There was a flurry in the water ahead of them. Several of the lights went out, and suddenly, another group of men swam toward them. As they got closer, their leader stopped and turned sideways and pointed to his arm, where the flag of the United States was clearly visible. The Professor's signal had worked. He had sent the code that they had found the treasure but were under attack, and a Navy Seal team immediately hit the water from the USS Carney, a destroyer on interdiction duty that had been moved to off the coast.

The team quickly gave portable breathing devices to the five men, whose lungs were near bursting. They put the Professor and Mack on motorized sleds and assisted the others, swimming with them to the Carney. Once there, they were lifted from the sea onto the deck and taken below, where the wounded received medical attention and the others were allowed to rest and recover.

CHAPTER 50

It is amazing what a hot shower, a hot meal, cold drinks, and a good night's rest can do. Jake, Mike, and Andre, feeling almost normal again after their ordeal, headed below deck to sick bay, where the Professor and Mack were resting under the ship's doctor's orders.

"Okay," said Mike as they entered, "you two don't look too bad."

"You guys look pretty good yourselves," said Mack. Then he looked straight at Andre. "Andre, thanks for saving our lives, man. That was a stand-up thing you did back there."

"Yu know how it be, mon. Me gotta tek care of de Professor here."

"Yeah, I know," said Mack, smiling. "Listen, Jake, what can you do to get me out of here?"

"Me, too," said the Professor. "I have many things to do. There's going to be years and years of work involved, salvaging and cataloging the treasure, and finding a suitable location for it to be displayed and . . ."

"Hold on right there, Professor," said Jake, "I have to interrupt you, and I have something I have to tell you."

The Professor had some inkling of what was coming and lie back on his pillow.

"What is it, Mr. Sullivan?"

"Last night, a large Navy Seal team was dispatched to the site of the warehouse, which had already been placed under control of an engineering team to shore up the remains of the cavern and warehouse and a guard team in submersibles to deny access to the site. They spent the night loading the treasure chests into propeller-driven underwater storage craft. The treasure was then taken out to sea and off-loaded onto an old rust bucket flying the Brazilian flag, which is now on its way to Key West, where the treasure will be unloaded at the Naval Air Station and then flown by military transport to Fort Knox, Kentucky, where it will remain until its final disposition can be determined."

"More work by your CIA, I presume," said the Professor. "How dare they! That treasure belongs to the Jamaican people! Your government had no right to confiscate it!"

"See, me tell yu dis," said Andre, "de bassmon git it all a de peoples git de shit!"

"Calm down, you two. I said the final disposition is to be determined. You know full well that Great Britain, Spain, Jamaica, and the United States are going to claim all or part of that fortune for themselves, and there's going to have to be some agreement worked out as to what finally happens to it. But for now, the key thing, so far as the United States government is concerned, is to ensure that it doesn't fall in the hands of ISIS or any other terrorist group or enemy of the United States."

The Professor was somewhat mollified.

"I see, Mr. Sullivan, and I do, to some degree, understand. But tell me, when will this disposition take place?"

"I can't tell you that, Professor. I have a feeling that it's going to take some time, given all the parties involved, but I promise you I will do my best to see that the people of Jamaica are treated fairly."

"I have your word, Mr. Sullivan?"

"You do," said Jake.

"That's sufficient for me."

"Me tink yur word be good, Jake Sullivan, but me tell yu . . . yu give de trut to dis mon, here. He be deservin' dat."

Just then, an ensign appeared in the doorway.

"Mr. Sullivan, Mr. Bates' chopper has landed and he wants to see the three of you."

"That man's always ruining the fun," said Mike.

"All right," said Jake. "You two rest. We'll get this all sorted out."

After they were gone, the Professor turned to Mack Owens.

"Mr. Owens, there's something else I'd like to discuss with you, if I may."

"Sure, Professor. What is it?"

And Professor Dixon proceeded to explain his request.

CHAPTER 51

The three men were directed to the ship's conference center, where Jason Bates was waiting.

"Glad to see you all made it through," said Bates. "I understand the Professor and Mr. Owens are doing well?"

"They'll be all right," said Mike, "although we do have a pissed off Professor and Andre on our hands."

"Why so?" asked Bates.

"Why do you think, Jason?" asked Jake.

"Ah . . . the distribution of the proceeds."

"Exactly," said Jake.

"He needs to be treated properly, Jason."

"Jake, come on. You know the political situation involved in this."

Andre spoke up, slamming his hand on the table.

"De politics be de bullshit! Dat mon found dis treasa . . . yu nanna treat him badly . . . yu unnerstan?"

"Jason," said Mike, "I know you always say there's politics, and I understand. But Andre is right. This guy, who most of the world probably would not have believed, had the good graces to come in contact with President Jordan Fletcher, who had the good sense to believe him. That man was the only one who could have found this treasure."

"As I understand it," said Bates, Mr. Sullivan had something to do with that, also."

"Just a lucky guess. The real effort was put forth by Professor Dixon," said Jake.

"I see," said Bates, smiling at Jake. "What is it you want me to do, Mr. Lang?"

"Well the way I see it, Jake and I have salvage rights to that treasure."

Surprised, Jake looked over at Mike.

"And we're claiming those rights."

"Yu two be de sons-of-bitches," yelled Andre, aghast at what Mike was saying.

"You can't be serious, Mr. Lang. You know you were working as an agent of the United States government at the time."

"I don't give a damn," said Mike. "I want part of the treasure," looking at Jake and smiling. Jake caught on.

"Yeah, he's right. We want part of the treasure."

"You, too?" asked Bates.

"Here's the deal, Jason . . . and there's no negotiations."

And Jake and Mike explained to the Chief of Staff of the President of the United States exactly what it was they wanted.

EPILOGUE

THE PIRATE CODE

CHAPTER 52

Two months later Jake Sullivan sat in his Miami Office, reading the latest story about "Morgan's Missing Millions" as the pundits were calling the treasure . . . well over five hundred million dollars, to be exact.

Just then, Mike came running into the office.

"We have a visitor," he said, as the elevator doors opened, just as Jake reached the entrance to the Justice Department office. Behind a squad of Secret Service Agents was Jordan Fletcher, President of the United States.

"Good day, gentlemen," he said. "I'm on my way to Jamaica to meet with their representative and representatives of Spain and Great Britain to determine the distribution of the treasure. Everybody and their cousin have filed claims."

"Just your usual international bullshit," said Mike.

"Exactly, Mr. Lang. At least we have ISIS on the run in Afghanistan. Allied air strikes have destroyed most of the poppy fields and they seem to have lost interest and are withdrawing their forces as we speak. Also, the Shower Posse is being rounded up by a joint task force of the DEA and the Narcotics Division of the Jamaican Constabulary. As you are aware, we couldn't keep Mack Owens from being part of it, and even with a sling, he is a formidable force. He and Superintendent Williams are reporting great success in disbanding the organization. Of course, it seems we have to worry about a new cartel trying to expand its power from Cuba into the old areas being vacated by Jamaica and Mexico . . . but, one day at a time. We'll deal with that as it comes."

"What about Damian Henry?" asked Jake.

"Completely disappeared off the face of the earth. No one can find him. No one is talking. We have no idea where he is."

"Well, gentlemen, I wanted to stop en route and thank you once again for your services. Seems I can always count on you to get the job done."

"Thank you, Mr. President."

"No . . . I thank you gentlemen," and with that, the President turned and started to walk away, and then turned back. "Oh, one other thing. I hear you two have added your names to the list of those making claims."

Jake and Mike looked at each other.

"Not really for ourselves, Sir," said Jake.

The President smiled.

"Mr. Bates has informed me of your non-negotiable demands."

"You see, Sir . . .," said Mike.

"Don't worry, Mr. Lang. I agree completely and will ensure that those demands are met."

"Thank you, Sir," they both said, as he entered the elevator and was gone.

"See how that works?" said Mike. "When you and I are equals . . . see how we can talk to even the President of the United States to get things done? That's the way it should always be."

"Uh-huh," said Jake, as he turned and walked away.

Mike followed after him.

"I'm serious."

CHAPTER 53

It took six months, but the powers that be finally arrived at an agreement. The United States, Great Britain, and Spain each received a one-quarter share of the treasure to do with as they saw fit, and they agreed to jointly administer a one-fourth share provided to Jamaica to ensure that it was used for educational and health purposes and creation of infrastructure on the island.

Additionally, the agreement proposed a standing special task force to be headed by the Jamaican Narcotics Division of the Constabulary Force of Jamaica, specifically Superintendent Antwon Williams, representing Jamaica, and Special DEA Agent Mack Owens representing the United States.

The agreement to which Jamaica was a signatory also held that if there was any evidence of governmental support of the Shower Posse or any other drug cartel, U.S. troop deployments would immediately be made to the island.

Additionally, as Jake and Mike had demanded, there was a special distributions made to Professor Dixon, who was the newly named head of the Jamaican Historical and Cultural Trust, to create a new state of the art headquarters to be built in Port Maria.

And finally, a separate, unannounced distribution was made to one Andre Powell for his services in recovering the treasure, as dictated by The Pirate Code.

CHAPTER 54

One year after their adventures in Jamaica, Mike and Jake were once again sitting on one of the balconies of the Casa Maria Hotel, talking and laughing with Mack Owens and Professor Dixon, still somewhat hobbled and using a cane. They had spent the afternoon at the dedication of the new Cultural and Historical Center, having been invited to attend by the Professor and his new assistant, Andre Powell.

It seems that Special DEA Agent Owens and Professor Dixon had reached an agreement themselves during their time in sick bay off the coast of Jamaica.

Professor Dixon was given custody of Mr. Powell during a probationary period agreed to by all the parties.

"Gentlemen, I know I keep saying this, but I cannot begin to thank you for what you have done for this island and me, personally."

"No need for thanks, Professor. It is all a result of your knowledge of and belief in this island," said Jake.

Finally, Andre arrived, bolted up the steps of the Casa Maria to the balcony where the four men were sitting, and went directly to Mack Owens.

"Me know me canna tek back wa me did," said Andre. "Me say me be sorry naah enough, but me tell you dis . . . me tank yu fa de chance, a me mek yu proud."

Mack got up and smiled and shook his hand.

"We've all done things in the past, Andre. Some were worse than others, but most everybody deserves a second chance. Make the best of it, son."

"Me will," said Andre. "Yu can place de bet on dat. Tank yu, too, Mr. Sullivan . . . Mr. Lang. Me feel bad 'bout callin' yu de names when de Bates talkin' to us. Yu two fix de whole ting fa de Professor."

"No problem, and thank you, Andre. You saved our lives when the water came roaring into that warehouse and Damian's men attacked. You stick with the Professor here and you'll be all right."

"Dat me know. Deh teacha . . . he deh bassmon, no doubt," and they all laughed.

"So, I hear you have the Posse on the run, Mack," said Jake.

"It's really been pretty easy. Without government sanctions, they are having great difficulty in operating."

"What about ISIS? They still trying to buy a cartel?" asked Mike.

"There's some renewed talk about Cuba, but they don't control the poppy fields anymore. The war is starting to turn against them in Syria, and they're having trouble fighting on two fronts. No doubt they're still out there, as vicious as ever, and they'll do anything they can to destroy us, so nothing will surprise me. We just have to keep after them. That's all we can do."

"Still no word on the head asshole, Damian Henry?" asked Mike.

"Vanished," said Mack. "Not a word. Not a trace. We've had some alleged sightings and nothing has panned out . . . but we'll find him. It's only a matter of time."

"Speakin' of de time," said Andre, "me got an appointment me gotta keep. Me see yu all de marrows befo yu tek de plane back, yeh?"

"We'll be here for breakfast," said Jake.

"Dat good," said Andre. "Me see yu den," and he headed to his car and drove off.

"You might have your work cut out for you, Professor," said Mike, pointing at the departing Andre.

"No, Mr. Lang. Andre will be fine . . . just fine."

CHAPTER 55

Andre stood in the Port Maria Cemetery at the base of the monument he had erected for Billy and his family, right next to the one he had bought for his father with the monies they had given him for his part in the discovery of the treasure. He spoke to his father first.

"Fadda, me was de bad mon. No doubt. But me do de right ting, a now me be de good mon, a will be. Me promise. Me mek yu proud. De Professor, he gonna teach me better to read a write a speak. Me gonna help Jamaica be de better place . . . teach de pickneys our history a wa we be 'bout. Yu see Fadda, yu be proud."

And then he spoke to Billy.

"Me found him, Billy, me knew me would. Me mek de promise to yu, a now me keep it. Me be so sorry, Billy . . . so sorry. It be me fault. Me hope yu can fagive me, 'cause me canna fagive meself."

He put his hand on the black marble monument where Billy's name was engraved, patted it, and turned and walked away.

CHAPTER 56

Andre slowly moved along the outside of the dilapidated house in the Denham Town slum outside of Kingston, the Glock 17 he had purchased from one of his former associates in his hand. He moved slowly to the back door and saw that it was slightly ajar. He could hear a television through the screen as he slowly pushed it open and entered., moving quietly toward the sound coming from a front room.

Holding the Glock in front of him, he was moving deeper into the house when a smell hit him, almost making him vomit as he wretched. He pushed open a swinging door that entered into the kitchen, and he gasped.

There sat Damian Henry in a straight-backed chair, taped at the wrists and ankles with dried blood in a pool around his feet. He was surrounded by flies and his body was bloated. Andre would not have recognized him, except for his head, which sat in his lap, his neck a bloody stump. The flag of ISIS was nailed to the wall behind him.

The gun hung at Andre's side as he turned and walked back the way he had come. Once outside, he bent over and vomited. Taking several deep breaths, he stood erect and looked up at a night sky full of stars.

"It be done, Billy," he said. "De bastard git de end he deserve. It be done."

CHAPTER 57

It had been a long day at the office and Jake had fallen into a deep sleep in the comfort of his bed. A ringing in the distance became louder, and half awake, he realized it was the phone.

Almost knocking the cell phone off of the nightstand, he recognized the number on the caller ID, the time showing as 3:58 A.M., and was instantly alert.

"Jake!" came the familiar voice.

"Linda? What is it? What's wrong? Are you and the girls all right?"

"Jake . . . it's Susan Branson. She's been murdered . . . and they've arrested Simon! Jake, you have to come home!"

COMING SPRING 2016

CHANGES IN
LATITUDES,
CHANGES IN
ATTITUDES

A JAKE SULLIVAN NOVEL

CHIP BELL

CHIP BELL

1725 FIFTH AVENUE
ARNOLD, PA 15068

724-339-2355

chip.bell.author@gmail.com
clb.bcymlaw@verizon.net
www.ChipBellAuthor.com

FOLLOW ME ON FACEBOOK
facebook.com/chipbellauthor

FOLLOW ME ON TWITTER
@ChipBellAuthor

FOLLOW ME ON PINTEREST
pinterest.com/chipbellauthor
/the-jake-sullivan-series

**TAKE THE TIME TO REVIEW
THIS BOOK ON AMAZON**
amazon.com/author
/chipbellauthor.com

WA